D0674146

B.

*Tom heard his own voice, hoarse, unrecognisable.
"You're a spy! Blackadder—you!"*

(*See page* 63)

BLACKADDER

by

JOHN KEIR CROSS

COLLINS

LONDON AND GLASGOW

First published in this edition 1961

PRINTED AND MADE IN GREAT BRITAIN BY
WM. COLLINS SONS AND CO. LTD.
LONDON AND GLASGOW

CONTENTS

INTRODUCTION
by
John Keir Cross

PART ONE
by
The Editor

PART TWO
by
Admiral Sir Thomas Cathro

PART THREE
by
Mr. Henry Rowan

CONTENTS

PART FOUR
by
The Editor

PART FIVE
by
Admiral Sir Thomas Cathro

ENVOI
by
The Editor

BEFORE YOU BEGIN

BLACKADDER is a story that I enjoyed writing; and it seems, from their flattering letters, that a great many people have enjoyed reading it. I hope that you will too.

Among these letters there have been several inquiries about how much of the story is based on fact; and perhaps I should explain here just how it was that this tale of adventure came into being.

I had written a serial play for the B.B.C. about life on Mars; and what we had tried to do in presenting it was to stick as closely as we could to the *probable* scientific truth. There were no ray-guns, no supermen, no fantastic escapades in some vague future: it was all as if the journey through space had actually happened and the people taking part in it had come to the radio studio to relate their experiences at first hand.

The method seemed to be very popular; and Lionel Gamlin, the producer of the serial, suggested that we might apply the same technique to an historical tale. At that time both he and I had been reading much about life in Britain in the days of Nelson; so we naturally chose that period for the new experiment—and decided too that we would introduce the great Admiral himself as one of the characters.

Thus BLACKADDER gradually took shape, written first as a book and then remoulded as a serial play. To follow out Lionel Gamlin's original scheme, I felt that it would be a help to cast parts of the book in the form of authentic-seeming manuscripts, written mainly by the two heroes of the adventure, Tom Cathro and Harry de Rohan, looking back in later life on the days when, as boys, they had come face to face with the arch-villain who almost destroyed them. And to fill in the parts of the tale that neither they nor the other narrators like Habbakuk McGuffie had touched on, I imagined an Editor, a writer of our own times, who had come across the old papers and set them in order. This man I called Stephen MacFarlane (he was, in fact, one of the characters in that previous play about space-flight that I have mentioned).

All this sounds very complex, and perhaps, if I were writing BLACKADDER anew, I would choose some other method. But since so many people have indeed found pleasure in the contrasting styles of the different narrators, and have felt the atmosphere stronger because of them, it has seemed wiser after all to leave the book exactly as it was first conceived.

But at least the historical backgrounds are all, I think, reasonably accurate, the account of Trafalgar in particular having been built from several genuine first-hand accounts of that great fight. And other authentic details crept into the story too as it took shape. There was indeed such a prison fortress as *La Grosse Tête*, for instance, where Tom and Harry are held captive by *La Vipère Noire*. In an old account of an escape attempt from it by some British Officers I came across the name "Lieutenant Butterfield"; so in a sense he at least was an historical personage (although I naturally invented all the rest of his adventures). It is true too that Napoleon was very interested in the possible use of balloons as weapons of war—he had even a plan at one time to carry out a "blitz" on London with fire-bombs, and to drop paratroops. And Butterfield's description of a flight in one of those primitive ships of the air is based fairly closely on an account of ballooning technique by an early aeronaut.

In short, as so often happens in writing, the tale of BLACKADDER is an amalgam of fact and fiction— indeed to such an extent that I hardly know myself, looking back, where one began and the other ended!

One final word: the play version of BLACKADDER would never have been the success it was—the whole story would never have seen the light at all, in fact— if it had not been for the encouragement and production skill of Lionel Gamlin. And so it is only fitting, I think, that this book should be dedicated to him; as it hereby is, in gratitude for all his help and in memory particularly of a morning in Broadcasting House when he and I, listening to a symphony of Kurt Atterberg which provided the "theme music" for the play, unmistakably saw the grey buildings of Portland Place melt all away, and beyond them had a glimpse of the great *Victory* herself, painted in yellow and black and with her flags a glory against the sky as she surged southwards on a September day long past to Cape Trafalgar.

J.K.C.: DEVON 1961

PART ONE

"ILL MET BY MOONLIGHT"

Being the first part of the history of BLACK-ADDER, his friends and his enemies, reconstructed from various fragments of old manuscript

by

The Editor

CHAPTER ONE

THE MONTH OF MAY

LONG AFTER it was all over, when he was an old man and a famous man—no less a personage than an Admiral of Her Majesty's Navy—Tom Cathro wrote in a letter to a friend:

"*I have seen much, I have done much; I have adventured in foreign lands and upon the high seas; I have been within a sight of death and wrestled with fear itself. But in all my long days of travel and travail I have known no such terror as gripped me in the heart long ago—long ago when I was a boy; and I encountered for the first time, face to face, the monstrous figure we knew as Blackadder. . . .*"

Thus he wrote; and so the tale is told: pieced together in this first part from the fragments of old diaries and letters and other scraps of writing which have come into my hands, and from gossip and hearsay in the village where Tom lived, and where his descendants still live—the village that was the headquarters of the dreaded Loblolly Boys, where the honest folk barred up their doors as the Moonshine went stealthily by—where to this day, they say, on stormy cloud-racked nights, the great, crooked, evil figure of Blackadder himself can still be glimpsed on the headland, his arms flung up to the sky, his white face twisted in an eternal rage. . . .

It began, Tom used to say, on an afternoon in May of the year 1803, which ever afterwards was known to him and his friend Harry de Rohan as the Terrible Year.

The weather had been a glory for days—it seemed high summer instead of spring. All England was in a burst of green—the trees shouted up to the sky in an ecstasy. But across the Channel at that very moment Napoleon was arming to attack—and all England knew it. After two uneasy years of peace, it was a matter of bare hours before war was declared again by one side or the other. On every village green in the land the militia were drilling—along the whole coast, from hilltop to hilltop, the beacons were ready, the lookouts stood at guard with telescopes drawn for a sight of the great fleet of barges mustered on the other shore. Rumours flew fast. There was wild talk of great clouds of balloons which Bonaparte would launch in a north wind and which would disgorge a hail of fire-bombs and grenades all over England. A tale went round that for many months the French had been digging ("like moudies," as old Mrs. Caithness said) at a tunnel beneath the very floor of the Channel itself—and when the moment came the last few feet of earth would burst and an angry horde debouch on our shores. There were stranger whispers of monstrous vessels which had been sighted off Boulogne—great hulking shapes, unmasted and billowing smoke; which could dive beneath the very surface of the sea itself and swim below like fishes, and so transport an evil submarine enemy to destroy us all invisibly. What could our own fleet do against such monsters?—what hope was there even in the famous Wooden Walls before such devil's devices? . . .

So the fever of excitement flew from one end of the country to the other. Block-houses and barricades were built at the approaches to every southern city. Heavy guns at practice near Dover sent the false news that the invasion had actually begun. The King himself, with seven of his sons in full battle array, paraded with the volunteers in the Capital. Arrangements were made to blow up the Thames bridges if Napoleon reached as far as London . . . and, at Portsmouth, on board his ship the *Victory*, Admiral Nelson consulted with his colleauges in a plan of campaign—a campaign which was to lead him, two years later, to Trafalgar and everlasting glory. . . .

But young Tom Cathro, that May afternoon, was concerned with nothing of the coming war. He was full of the excitement of the weather. Beyond the small cluster of houses—his mother's two-roomed cottage among them—the sea sparkled brilliantly in the sunshine. It seemed, unbelievably, warm enough to bathe. In the little village of Lytchett, in South Dorset, every able-bodied man and youth was hard at work digging trenches, or drilling before the church to the bellowed commands of old Squire Westwood, whose grandfather had fought at Malplaquet and who saw himself as a military genius in consequence. Tom was among the diggers—had been at it since early morning; but on a sudden impulse he threw down his spade and went running through the street.

"Where are you off to, Tom?" shouted huge Ben Corbin, the blacksmith, straightening himself, so that his great muscles rippled and glistened in the sun. He was stripped to the waist, as all the men were—as Tom himself was as he ran.

"To the sea," shouted Tom, over his shoulder. "I'm going for a swim!—I'll be back in an hour—less, maybe."

He darted into his mother's cottage for long enough to snatch up an old cloth to dry himself with, and to cram some bread and cheese into his waistband. Then he went on again, through the main street towards the house on the village outskirts where his friend Harry de Rohan lived.

As he went he passed Mr. Abershaw's cottage. At any other time he would have stopped for a word or two with this genial old friend of his who had come to settle in the village some years before, but he was too full of his sudden desire for a swim to want to stop on this occasion. The old man was standing in his garden, however, and as he saw Tom he gave a cheery wave.

"Good day, Tom," he called, smiling. "Fine weather, fine weather!"

His tall lean figure, dressed in its perpetual black, even on such a day, was a strange contrast against the lilac blossom. All round him fluttered a cloud of the pigeons he loved so deeply—they swooped down from the tall cotes to land on his shoulder or to peck for a moment at the bread·and seeds he held out to them on his outstretched hand.

"Where are you off to?" he called again. "You're in a hurry, boy, surely!"

"To the sea, sir," Tom called back. "To swim."

"To swim? It's early enough in the year for that yet, surely?"

"The first of the season. I don't expect we'll stay in for long—'twill be too cold for that, I guess. But the sun's warm enough at least."

"Take care you meet with none of Boney's folk," the old man smiled. "It's the very day for them. I warrant it's this turn of the weather they've been waiting for, or the war would have broken long since. They say our Ambassador's left Paris already—they say Napoleon insulted him wickedly at a public assembly."

"War or not it's the sea for me," Tom called, making to run on. "Any case, if the Frenchies do invade they'll never aim to land here. 'Twill be further along the coast, I reckon—never in Dorset."

"Oh, strange things *can* happen in Dorset, my boy," Mr. Abershaw answered, with another wave of his hand. And, then, with Tom almost out of hearing: "Will you be in to see me later, perhaps?—you and your friends, Tom? For some music, perhaps?"

"Perhaps. Later on—in the evening maybe. We'll come in in the evening, perhaps. . . ."

And on he went, the cloth which he had wrapped

round his neck flapping out in the little breeze blowing in from the shore. He made a mental note to remember to call in on Mr. Abershaw when the digging was done for the day. He and Harry visited him often, and always enjoyed themselves enormously. The old man was a retired music-master from London, where, the rumour went, he had been very famous in his earlier days. The little cottage in Lytchett was full of curios —rare old books, strange carvings that Mr. Abershaw had picked up all over Europe in his early travels, whole drawers of ancient fire-arms, which the old man had made a hobby of collecting and so on. He had endless tales of the lands he had visited, and if Tom was not particularly fond of music, Harry was, and sat completely entranced when Mr. Abershaw took up the flute which had been his favourite instrument in other times and played old airs to them. And at the end of it all, on these visits, there was always a glass of mulled ale and a slice of shortcake for the boys, while Mr. Abershaw sat with his glass of fine old brandy, beaming at them as he sipped it—

"—but don't ask me where I have it from," he would say. "I may be retired from the world long since, and see few folk these times but yourselves, lads; but I still have a friend or two here and there whose names I won't mention, and who leave me a little keg at the door some nights as the Moonshine goes through the village on its way to the north. . . ."

And he would wink and raise his glass to them; and Tom and Harry would thrill at the mention of the deadly word, and draw closer for a moment to the fire; and recall the nights when they lay in their beds at home—the nights when the sign had gone up that the Loblolly Boys were to be out and all the cottage doors to be locked. And, as they lay there alert and unsleeping, there would come the soft muffled tramp of feet through the fields behind the houses, with perhaps a stealthy command or two in the still night air; and if they crept to their windows to peep out they would see the dim anonymous shapes go creeping through the mist all laden with kegs and boxes and baskets, and the moonlight would gleam on the upraised barrel of a gun or the ready blade of a sabre— and perhaps, for all they knew, that very night would bring destruction to some indiscreet traveller who did not know the sinister rules of the game and had inadvertently come face to face with the Loblollies and so would recognise them again—and so was dangerous —and so was dead. . . .

Only once, on one such night long before, had Tom glimpsed for a moment the dreaded shape—as he believed—of the leader of the Loblollies himself. On a Moonshine night he had slid to his bedroom window, crouching shivering below the sill so that his white face would not betray him. He heard the steady swishing of the smugglers' boots in the long grass of the meadow beyond the cottage. Stealthily he raised his head to peep through a crack in the half-closed shutter at the side of the window. And below him, suddenly clear in a parting of the swirling ground-mist, was a tall still figure. In the silence, in the moonlight, there was, as it seemed, an emanation from that quiet unmoving shape of utter evil: whoever he was, the man before him—the leader of the vast secret organisation which had terrorised the countryside round Lytchett for many, many months—whoever he was, he was a man not to be crossed, a man who would stop at nothing to gain his own foul ends.

In the sudden instinctive sense of danger from the figure below, Tom drew back with a sharp intake of breath; and as he did so his elbow brushed against a chair in the corner of the bedroom, which over-toppled and fell to the floor. In an instant the figure beneath started and half-turned. He made to draw the great sabre at his waist and the moonlight flashed on the partly-drawn blade. Tom had a glimpse, imper-fect and indistinct, of a white thin face beneath the black tricorne the King of the Smugglers wore. The lower part of the face was wrapped in a dark cloth, but he glimpsed the eyes, and they burned wickedly towards his window. He stayed perfectly still, his heart pound-ing furiously, terrified lest he should be seen—for it was death to be seen, for man or woman or child. But the figure beneath, after staying poised for a moment, as suddenly turned away again, sheathing the great sabre as he did so. From across the fields had come the low, repeated call of an owl, which was plainly a signal of some kind; and with a sudden movement the King of the Smugglers plunged forward into the mists and was swallowed up and hidden from Tom's view.

His heart still beating painfully, Tom crept back to bed. "Blackadder," he whispered, "Blackadder . . .

Blackadder himself! ..." And he shivered a little again as he lingered over the dreaded name.

"Blackadder himself! ... Ah! if I had seen his face —if only I had seen his face! If only I knew what all the world wants to know! And yet ... thank heaven I did not, after all! ..."

CHAPTER TWO

THE COVE

THAT AFTERNOON in May when the story begins, Tom found his friend Harry de Rohan in the garden of his house beyond the village. He was helping his grandfather tend the flower beds. Both figures straightened themselves as Tom approached, the one small, slight, but with an impression of immense vitality in it, the other tall and dignified, the personification of the old aristocracy from which it had sprung.

Harry was delighted at Tom's suggestion for a swim.

"May I, grandpère?" he asked. "Only for a little while, I promise—and we won't stay in for long."

"It will still be very cold, I fancy," said the old man doubtfully. "Still, you know I can deny you nothing, my dear child, and so you must go if you wish. Only you must be careful—you must promise that you will be careful. Tom—you are the slightly older: undertake that you will not let him venture too far. He is all I have in the whole world—there is nothing else left to me."

Tom nodded, touched as he always was by the gentle manner of the old aristocrat. The Chevalier de Rohan spoke English perfectly, with only the smallest trace of accent. He had said himself, many years before, that the least he could do was to learn to speak correctly the language of the country that had adopted him; and so he had taken infinite pains to master all the complexities of our tongue. If anything, he spoke perhaps a little overcarefully, using an occasional word or phrase which might have seemed unusual in the mouth of a born Englishman. But this aside, and one or two aspects of manner, the Chevalier, a refugee from the Revolution in France so many years before, might well have passed for an old-style Dorset gentleman of the previous century.

As for his grandson, he had spent nearly all his days in England, and so had no trace at all of his French ancestry. His very name had been changed from the French Henri to the English Harry; and already in some parts of the county the English version of his other name was being used. The French "de" was being dropped, the inhabitants of the old manor house at the southern end of Lytchett were being referred to simply as the "Rowans."

In a few moments the two boys were ready to set off. They ran forward towards the sea, waving back as they went to the old man in the garden.

"I like your grandfather, Harry," said Tom. "There's something so . . . oh, I don't know!—kind of helpless about him, somehow. You feel you want to be looking after him all the time—wondering what you can do for him maybe."

"It's how I feel about him too," said Harry with a smile. "I think it's because he had such terrible experiences in the old times, you know. He never mentions them much—only occasionally, usually when it comes round to the anniversary of the time my mother and father were killed—next month that is, as a matter of fact. I know he thinks a lot about those old days—when he was a kind of prince in France, you know—before the Revolution."

"It must be strange for him to look back on it. Everything has changed so terribly for him."

"Well, the only way to think of it is that he and I are lucky to be alive at all, Tom," said Harry. "We might have been guillotined too, the way my mother and father were—that was what was meant to happen, you know."

"They'd never have guillotined you, Harry—surely. You were only what?—two or so. You were no more than a baby."

"Oh, they'd have got rid of me some other way, perhaps—but they'd certainly have guillotined my grandfather. They were determined to wipe out all our family—every one of us. If he and I hadn't escaped there would be no de Rohans left by now—not one—not of our branch of the family at any rate. I'm the last of the line—and that's why grandfather is so determined to take good care of me. It's a bit embarrassing at times, of course—if he had his way I'd never be allowed to do anything at all except sit safely indoors. Still, I can usually handle him. . . ."

By this time they had almost reached the beach. Suddenly, running towards them from the dunes to the right, which hid a little isolated group of cottages, they saw a girl of about their own age.

"It's Phil," cried Harry. "Hullo, Phil. We're off for a swim. Are you coming?"

"I'll come with you, if you like," said the girl breathlessly, drawing up with them. "I'll watch you, at any rate. I'm not coming in—it's too cold."

"Tush, it's as hot as midsummer!" smiled Tom.

"Maybe—the sun is at least. But I wager it isn't the same in the sea. I'll watch your clothes if you want."

They went on together, towards the little cove where they usually bathed. Phil was the daughter of a foreshore fisherman and her full name was Philadelphia—Philadelphia Wentworth—"just about the stupidest name I ever heard," as she said herself. "Still, there's always been a Philadelphia in the family since ever anyone can remember—'twas my mother's name, and her mother's name and hers before that and so on and so on, right back to the beginning. So I reckon I just must put up with it—and anyhow, it can be shortened to Phil, and there's nothing wrong with that for a name. . . ."

"I saw you coming down from Harry's house from my window," she went on to explain now. "I reckoned you'd be aiming to bathe when I saw the towels you had round your necks, so I thought I'd better come out and warn you."

"Warn us," said Tom. "About what?"

"Oh, not to stay in too long, perhaps."

"We weren't going to. It'll be too cold for that. Only a quick swim and then out. Oh, by the way, Harry—I meant to tell you. Mr. Abershaw wants us to go in this evening—later on a bit maybe. I said we might, if you're not doing anything."

"Nothing at all—I'd love to go. There's nothing I like better than a chat with the old boy."

"Better not stay too late with him either, then," persisted Phil darkly. "Better not go at all, in fact. If I were you I'd go straight home and stay there after you've had your swim. Anyway, I'm not going to old Abershaw's with you, even if you ask me."

"I was, as a matter of fact," said Tom. "You usually want to come with us. What's the trouble this time? Afraid to walk home in the dark afterwards?—we'll come with you, if that's what's bothering you."

"No thank you! Even if you did come with me I reckon I'd still be afraid—to-night leastways. I suppose you haven't heard yet?"

"Heard what?"

"Oh, the Loblollies—that's all."

"What—to-night?"

"To-night as ever is. The word hasn't gone all round yet, but it will. The sign's up, leastways—on the old signpost near the harbour, same as usual. A newly-killed adder. Father came in about ten minutes ago and told mother—and he said she was to start spreading the word round all the village. He was very excited—he always is when the sign goes up."

"Maybe he's one of the Loblollies himself," said Tom. "You never know—anyone might be. Does he go out on Moonshine nights, Phil?"

"Maybe does—I don't know. They always send me to bed upstairs and I keep my head under the clothes on Moonshine nights. Maybe Father is one—I know Ben Corbin the Blacksmith is."

"How do you know?"

"Oh, just guessed. Haven't you ever noticed that Mrs. Corbin has some new little thing to wear after a Moonshine night?—maybe a little bit of a lace collar, perhaps. She always has, and I reckon Ben gives it her as part of the spoils."

"Is lace one of the things they smuggle?" asked Harry.

"They smuggle anything they can make money from—and there must be plenty of sale in London and such-like for good French lace," said Philadelphia.

"It must be a risky business smuggling at a time like this," said Harry. "What about the war?"

"Oh, the war hasn't been declared yet—they'll go on right up to the last minute running things backwards and forwards across the Channel. In fact, I don't suppose that even if war does break out it will make a great deal of difference. The Loblollies will go on running just the same—at least some of them will."

" It would be trading with the enemy then."

"Suppose it is? Smuggling still went on before the peace, you know—it didn't make any difference at all—at least not much. I remember old Mrs. Webb telling me that her son was killed by the coastguards in a raid one night during the war. He used to slip across to France regular at nights and trade with them—and the very men he traded with were enemy soldiers and sailors during the day, like as not—same as he and the others were over here."

"That was before the Loblollies began, though."

"Of course it was—Josh Webb was killed four years ago and the Loblollies have only been working for two. But I bet it won't make much difference to them either—they're too well organised. . . ."

By this time they had reached the cove—a small, rockbound inlet in the main coastline of the huge bay. At high tide it was completely inaccessible from the shore itself—it could only be approached from the cliff-tops by means of a steep rock path. At the moment, however, the tide was low, and the three friends had reached the cove by way of the shore. Within it, they were completely cut off from view; to their right, beyond an outjutting shoulder of rock, lay the long beach stretching for perhaps a mile and a half to the tiny Lytchett Harbour; to their left, but hidden from view by another shoulder, was a continued line of high cliffs running on for some miles towards Poole.

Phil took up a modest position behind a boulder while the two boys prepared for their swim.

"It's all right," she called, "I won't look till you're in the water, and if you give me a shout when you're to come out I'll come behind the boulder again! "

Harry took a little longer than Tom to undress, for he had been more fully clothed. But it was only a few moments before they were both racing across the sand to the water.

"Ugh! It is cold," said Tom, as he plunged in. "Reckon old Abershaw was right—it's a bit too early yet. There hasn't been enough sun to warm the sea."

"One quick swim and we've done it," said Harry. "Come on, Tom—I'll race you to the Teeth."

The Teeth were half-a-dozen ragged and pointed rocks which thrust in a little line out into the sea beyond the left-hand shoulder of the cove. In an instant the boys were heading for them manfully, Tom slightly in the lead. He swam well, rejoicing in the feel of the water against his body after the first bitter shock of the coldness of it. Behind him he could hear Harry's excited spluttering as he struggled to make up to him, and so he redoubled his own efforts and reached the Teeth a few feet ahead of the other.

"My race," he gasped, as he pulled himself up the slippery side of the largest of the rocks. "See if you can do better on the way back."

Harry drew himself up beside him, and so they stayed for a moment, shaking the water from their hair and waving to Phil as she stood on guard beside their clothes.

"We're coming back and then straight out," shouted Harry to her. "You'd better get back behind your boulder again when you see us getting close to the shore. . . . Ready, Tom? "

"All ready," said Tom, poising himself for the plunge. But at the moment when he was about to dive forward he felt Harry's cold hand on his arm.

"Wait, Tom—wait! Look!—look there! "

He looked down to where his companion was pointing; and, in a hollow in the rock close to their feet, swaying to and fro a little in the slight swell of the rock pool where it lay, he saw a small black barrel—

no more than a keg; but curiously sinister somehow in its gentle rolling movement, as if it were the live trunk of an animal struggling ponderously and leglessly to heave itself up from its prison. . . .

"What about it?" he asked. "It's only an old staved keg of some kind, surely."

"I'll tell you what about it!" said Harry seriously, his teeth chattering together a little in the cold from the water as they stood there. "It's a sign! It's more than a staved-in keg, Tom—that thing there is more than only that. It's a sign that we aren't the only ones who have ever thought of using this cove because it's so out of sight."

"You mean—Blackadder's people! The Loblollies, Harry?"

"It's a Moonshine keg, if ever there was one. And it's been dropped here and left here from the last time they were out. . . . Tom, do you see what it means! Phil was right when she said we shouldn't stay too long in the cove! It's here they land—at the Teeth here. They'll be here to-night—just here, landing more! It's the very place for them—they can bring the boats right in, under the cliffs, and carry the stuff up over the rock path to the top. This is where they come, Tom—just here! . . ."

They stayed perfectly still for a moment, the cold forgotten as they stared down at the small black shape still rolling to and fro.

"Let's go back," said Tom quietly. " You're right— I should have spotted it myself. Harry, what should we do? Suppose it is here?—suppose this *is* where they land? Should we tell the coastguards? "

"I don't know. I suppose so. And yet they say the guards have all been bribed—they say that's why Blackadder is never taken on these trips of his—all the guards are in it too, they say. . . . We'll have to think it out, Tom—we must. Let's go back now—and we'd better not say anything to Phil—not till we've had a chance to talk it over. Come on—don't let's race this time. Let's get out and dress as quickly as we can."

They turned and plunged into the sea; and this time, in the sudden sense of menace that the thought of Blackadder had conjured up in them, the water seemed colder even than before as they swam back to the beach.

CHAPTER THREE

AN OLD TALE RETOLD

THEY DRESSED quickly and in silence and a few moments later were heading for the village again with Philadelphia beside them.

"You're very quiet," she said. "I suppose it was even colder than you thought it would be, only you don't want to admit it. Well, you would go for a swim in May!"

They made no answer and a moment later she went on:

"By the way, Harry, I hope you don't mind my asking. I couldn't help noticing while you were dressing —just before you got your shirt on. Is it some kind of tattoo mark you have on your chest?"

"Yes, it is," said Harry gruffly.

"Seems a strange thing for you to have—not what you'd expect somehow, is it, Tom? I mean, you ain't fisherfolk stock, or sailor stock of any kind, Harry."

"It was done a long while ago—an old sailor did it just after grandfather and I came down here to Dorset. I don't know why—it was some idea of grandfather's own. He was a little bit . . . well, strange after we escaped from France—he wasn't quite right in the head, I think—it had all affected him too deeply."

"What exactly did happen, Harry?—you've never really told me, you know."

"Oh, it's too long a story—really it is, Phil. I'll tell you some other time—not now."

"Why not now?—there's nothing else to talk about, is there?"

Harry, remembering the black keg in the hollow of the rocks, was about to say that there was, but he thought better of it.

"Well, all right—if you really want to know," he said with a sigh. "You see, before the Revolution over in France, grandfather was enormously wealthy. The de Rohans were a very old family—one of the oldest in all France—grandfather has told me we were descended from the ancient Kings and Dukes of Brittany, you know, and if you read any of the history books you'll find de Rohans cropping up over and over again. We weren't the main line of the family, but we were an important branch all the same, and we had huge estates and a kind of palace at a place called Rohan-Soubise not far from Paris."

"Do you remember what it was like, Harry?" interrrupted Phil eagerly. "I reckon it was very grand, and you had coaches and horses, and silk sheets on the beds and everything."

"I suppose we did," smiled Harry. "But I was far too young when we still lived there to be able to remember anything at all. I was only a baby—hardly a year old, in fact, when we had to leave."

"Why had you? The Revolutionaries?"

"Yes. The Sansculottes."

"That's what you were this afternoon," giggled Phil. "I know enough French for that, anyway. It means ' without-trousers ', doesn't it? "

"It was used to mean the rougher kind of Revolutionaries—the ones who were out to destroy the old aristocratic families at any price. At the start of the Revolution we were left fairly well alone—the people on our estate had always been decently cared for. Grandfather had never belonged to the old school of aristocrats who ruled by oppression, and he'd brought up my father in the same way. My father was his only son, you know—and he was married not long before the beginning of the Revolution itself. I was born in 1789, just when the Revolution started—at Rohan-Soubise. . . ."

And so he went on, as they walked homewards. Tom had heard some fragments of the story before, but never the whole thing from its start to its finish. He listened quietly, swinging his towel against the roadside grasses and occasionally asking a question as Harry perhaps hesitated and seemed as if he might want to stop as some aspect of the old adventure grew too painful in its recollection.

This, in its essence, is the story that gradually pieced itself together as Harry talked:

As the Revolution in France built up to its climax of the Reign of Terror, it became clear that the more fanatical of the Sansculottes would want to destroy the family of the de Rohans just as surely as they aimed to destroy all the other old aristocratic families.

The Chevalier had secret information from a friend in Paris that a move was to be made to arrest them, and so made instant arrangements to try to get his son and daughter and their infant son—the last of the line— out of the country to England. They set off from Rohan-Soubise by coach late one night, the old man disguised as a travelling wine-merchant on his way to England for orders, his son as his junior partner. Harry's mother was said to be travelling with them for her health—they had even managed to get a certificate from a doctor friend to say that she needed sea air and a change of climate.

They reached the coast in safety and were waiting for a boat when some soldiers from Paris arrested them —the plot had been discovered and they had been pursued.

They were taken back to Paris and put in prison— the Conciergerie. There was a mockery of a trial, and the fact that they had tried to escape told heavily against them. They were condemned to death—even Harry, young as he was; and sent back to prison—this time La Force—to await the carrying out of the sentence.

There they were kept for many months, until they began to think that they had been forgotten. The conditions under which they lived were abominable— the food was bad, they had no opportunity for exercise. But gradually Harry's mother grew friendly with the wife of one of the gaolers. The woman took pity on them because of the baby, and managed to get permission for the whole family to take the air occasionally in the prison yard.

Through this woman, too, Harry's father contrived to make secret contact with some friends outside— notably the agent of the old Rohan-Soubise estate, a man named Bonnet. As the months went by, a plan of escape was gradually arranged between them. In the corner of the prison yard there was a small wicket gate which was kept heavily locked; but the Chevalier de Rohan succeeded in getting a wax impression of the key from the gaoler, and had it passed out to Bonnet so that a duplicate could be made. It was arranged that one day, when the family was exercising, the gate should be unlocked from the outside, and at a moment when the yard was deserted the de Rohans should slip quietly through. Beyond the prison wall there was only a deserted side-street, and it was unlikely that they would be seen there either. They would then be hurried across to a house opposite, which Bonnet had rented for the purpose, and there their prison clothes would be changed for the kind of costume that ordinary Revolutionaries might wear. They would come out from the house and mingle with the crowds, making their way across Paris to where Bonnet had found accommodation for them with a group of sympathetic Englishmen who would arrange for their passage across the Channel.

All went according to plan—at the outset at least. But as they made their way to join the Englishmen they were caught up in a crowd of revolutionaries—one of the innumerable crowds of half-crazed Parisians scouring the streets in those days singing revolutionary songs and looking for aristocrats in hiding. The mob did not know who they were, of course, or they would have been destroyed on the spot; but before they could get out of the way, they were swept up in the seething torrent and hurled forward. Harry was being carried on his grandfather's shoulder. The old man was thrust aside and fell against a wall—and if Bonnet had not caught the boy in time he would have been crushed to death. The other two—Harry's mother and father —were seized in the middle of the turmoil and swept instantly out of sight.

The old Chevalier was heavily stunned from his fall, coming as it had on top of all the excitement of the escape. But somehow the faithful Bonnet struggled with him, and got both him and Harry to the house where their sympathisers were waiting. There they stayed for some days, hoping against hope that the others might be able to join them, for they had been told the address and there was just the chance that if they succeeded in escaping from the mob they would be able to make their own way across Paris. But they did not come; and at the end of three days Bonnet learned that they had been recognised by one of the informers of La Force who had been with the crowd that day, and so had been taken back to prison.

For a week the old Chevalier lay desperately ill. He had no further wish to escape himself—he wanted only to go back to prison to join his son and daughter. But onnet persuaded him that his duty lay with Harry—

the boy was the last of the line of the de Rohans, and had to be protected at all costs. And at last, on the evening of the very day when, as they discovered afterwards, Harry's mother and father were guillotined, their English friends smuggled them both out of Paris to the coast—successfully this time—and so they reached England, and were taken to London. . . .

"And that's all," said Harry abruptly. " That's all the story. We stayed in London for a spell until grandfather's health improved. He had managed to bring some of the family jewels with him, and he was able to realise some money on them—enough for him to invest in a little wine-merchant's business, so that we both would have a living pension. But he didn't want to live in a city—he hated crowds and busy streets; so when one of his business friends told him he had a house for sale down here in Lytchett and he could have it cheaply, he decided to come and settle in it. That was nine years ago—almost ten; and we've been here ever since, as you both know. . . ."

He fell silent. They had reached the gate of the house itself by this time, and looking in towards it Harry saw the tall stooped shape of the Chevalier de Rohan at one of the windows. The old man smiled and nodded, waving to them; and Harry waved back, signalling that he would be in in a moment.

"I must go," he said. "He always worries if I stay out too long—he's terrified lest anything should happen to me—as the last of the line, you know. . . . Shall I see you later, Tom? "

"I was going to ask. You won't forget we've to go

to Mr. Abershaw's. And besides, there's—there's the other thing. . . ."

"I won't forget. I'll meet you at what?—six o'clock, say—in about an hour. Outside Mr. Abershaw's house. Look—there's one of those pigeons of his, do you see? —flying in from the sea. And another of them—look. Strange how fond he is of them—those and his music. All he cares about, it seems. They're coming home, I expect—it'll soon be dusk."

"Perhaps the pigeons know what night it is," said Phil with a nervous little smile. "They'll have seen the adder on the notice-board and will know it's a Moonshine night. I must go home myself before it gets dark."

"There's plenty of time yet," said Tom smiling. "They never walk till late, the Loblollies. It's ten o'clock at the earliest before Blackadder stirs."

"I hate that name," Phil said softly, with a sudden little shudder. "Oh, I just hate it! I don't know why . . . It's so—evil, somehow—it sounds all full of evil . . . . I wonder who he really is?"

"The King of the Smugglers? Who knows? He might be anyone—his real name might be Blackadder itself—he might be a stranger to the whole district who only comes down here on Moonshine nights. I wonder why we all think he must be someone we know?"

"I don't know. I just have a feeling that he *is*. . . . Tom, that time you saw him—the time you told me about once. . . . Did you see his face?"

"Not clearly," said Tom slowly. "It was half

muffled in a cloth—and the light was indistinct. But I had a notion that I had seen it before somewhere—there was something all about him that was familiar."

"Was he young or old?"

"Young. He seemed quite young. Too young to be what he was."

"He's more than just a smuggler, you know, Tom. I feel that in my bones. Smugglers are nothing—there have been smugglers in Lytchett since ever I remember —and my mother has told me about the smugglers in her time too. Almost all the old Lytchett men have done some smuggling at one time or another. But not this way—not this terrible secret way, and killing people if they see them, and making the folk all lock their doors up on Moonshine nights. . . . There's more in it than smuggling—it's not only Moonshine, Tom. There's more in it—it's something evil—something terribly evil. . . ."

"I feel that too," said Tom slowly. "I felt it that night—it was why I was so afraid that night. . . . Phil, you must keep quiet about that night, you know— you mustn't tell anyone that I have seen Blackadder, even indistinctly. If he were to find out—I mean, suppose he *is* someone we know—someone in the village here. . . . You know what it would mean. . . ."

"I won't tell anyone, Tom—I promise. Oh, I *must* get home!—look, the sky's clouding."

And she turned to go. But Harry, on a sudden thought, held her back.

"Wait, Phil. We forgot what it was that started me

telling all that old story of mine. The tattoo mark. It was done just after we came down to Lytchett here —there was an old seaman who used to do some gardening for us, and grandfather had the idea that he should do it. He was still not quite himself when we did leave London. It's the crest of the de Rohans, you know—at least, that's part of it; and there's a queer extra kind of device too, woven in with it. He drew it out for the old man to copy. He said something to me once about it being the old crest—the original of them all—in one of the rooms at our old palace of Rohan-Soubise. It was a queer notion—unlike him somehow, against all his instincts. I often think he regrets that he did have it done—he never mentions it. It was only a sudden whim, I think—because of his illness. He said once, when he did talk about it, that he had a notion that he wanted me never to forget that I was a de Rohan, even although we had renounced all our old ties. And so it was tattooed above my heart —so that I never would forget."

He pulled his shirt aside at the neck, and Tom and Philadelphia found themselves looking at the strange, compact, brightly-coloured little design against the white of his skin: a two-headed eagle encircled by a wreath of myrtle leaves and transfixed through the breast with a poignard, dripping blood. Behind this main design was an arrangement of crooked lines, wandering all round the figure in a complex maze; and above and below were some words in ancient French which neither could read.

Phil shuddered.

"It's—it's rather frightening, somehow," she said. "Did it hurt, Harry?—when it was done?"

"A little. I remember it did, just a little. But that's all past, years and years ago. And whether it's frightening or not, it's there for the rest of my life, Phil. There's nothing that can ever be done to take it away. I remember the old seaman telling me that at the time. He's dead now, poor old soul. He went back to sea when the first war broke out and he was killed at the Battle of the Nile. Old Corbin, it was—Ben Corbin's father, the blacksmith."

"And one of the Loblolly boys into the bargain, according to Phil," smiled Tom. "Well, if he is, and if it is a Moonshine night, he won't be digging any more trenches on the common—so I'll take my chance on not going there myself. I'll see you later, Harry—outside Mr. Abershaw's. Come on, Phil—I'll walk home with you if you like."

He took her arm and set off with her. Harry stood for a moment smiling after them, then, with one more quick glance at the strange design on his breast, wrapped his shirt round his neck again and went into the house to where his grandfather was waiting for him.

CHAPTER FOUR

AN AIR BY HAYDN

MR. ABERSHAW was playing the flute when the two boys arrived to visit him. They could hear him as they passed along the garden path, the low sweet sounds of the air mingling pleasantly with the throaty cooing from the dovecotes above. The melody was Mr. Abershaw's favourite, the tune above all others that he returned to over and over again: a little simple serenade by Haydn.

"I played it once for Haydn himself," Mr. Abershaw would say. "I knew him—I met him in London when he lived there. Ten years ago—more than ten; let me see . . . ninety-one, it was—seventeen ninety one. Ah, time passes, time passes! We shall never see such days again, when all the fashionable world used to flock to see the old master at his lodging, lads—and he was only the son of an Austrian wheelwright. But there was music in him, great music, and it raised him up above all others. He was a kind of angel, I think—not a man as we are. He opened his heart and God sang to us through it! . . ."

And then he would sigh, and hum a snatch of the air again, and take a pinch of snuff.

"Well, well, I may see him again someday—who knows. He still lives. When all these troubled times are over I shall make the pilgrimage to Austria, perhaps, and see old Papa Haydn—and perhaps he may let me play the serenade to him again, and he will smile, and pat my shoulder as he did last time when I played it in London long ago. And he'll say: *Gut—gut, little Abbie! Ah—sehr gut! . . .*"

The old man stopped in the middle of a phrase when he heard Tom and Harry at the door. His mules slip-slopped along the corridor and there was a deal of fumbling with chains and padlocks before he opened the door to them.

"Come in, come in, my dear young friends!" he cried, holding his arms out wide as if to embrace them. "Ah, I hardly thought you would come—you were so excited about your swim, Tom, when I asked you! I thought perhaps you would forget."

Chuckling delightedly and rubbing his thin long hands together, he led them through to the main room of the cottage.

"I'm glad—so glad. It's lonely for an old man like me in the evenings here—even although it was solitude I set out to find when I first came south. Sit down, sit down. You didn't bring Miss Philadelphia with you?"

"She wouldn't come, sir," said Tom. "I did ask her—she likes coming to see you as much as we do. But she said she was a little afraid to-night—she didn't want to have to walk home in the dark, even if one of us went with her. It's—it's a Moonshine night. Did you know, sir?"

The old man had seated himself before them, beside his music stand and was fingering his flute absently.

Now suddenly his face grew serious. "Yes—yes. . . . A Moonshine night. How sinister that lovely word has become! My neighbour from along the way came in to warn me—she said the sign had gone up this afternoon—the newly-killed adder on the signpost. . . . It's horrible—it's all so horrible."

He shuddered, then brightened with a small nervous smile.

"It was why I had the door so heavily locked, Tom —because I knew it was to be a Moonshine night. I hadn't fully expected you, you see—although I did half hope, and I've set the things all ready for your usual refreshment, do you see."

"You know who some of the Blackadder people are, don't you, sir?" asked Harry slowly. "I remember you told us. Some of them sometimes leave something for you at the door as they pass, I think you once said."

"Yes—yes, my boy. I do—I know who two of them are. But perhaps the less that's said of it the better. I learned quite accidentally, you see—not long after I came to settle here from London. I wish I never had."

"It usually means death to know," said Tom soberly. "Even accidentally."

"I know—I know, Tom. And that is why I do say so little about it. It so happened, you see, that I was able to do these two smugglers a service—these what do they call themselves?—Loblollies. . . . It was in the early days, when it was all just beginning—before their organisation had grown quite so big. And one night, when some of them were landing the contraband, the coastguards came down and raided them. These two men were wounded, and they came to my door for shelter—and you see, it was impossible for me to turn them away. So I hid them till the guards went past, and I tended their wounds. When they went they made me swear that I would never disclose to anyone who they were—and they swore in their turn that they would never tell their leader that it was I who had looked after them that night and so knew them. I think that if he did know——"

He hesitated; and a sudden flicker of fear went across his face. His long hands trembled as they caressed the flute.

"Do you mean that even if he knew you had saved their lives Blackadder would have you . . . killed, sir?" asked Tom.

"I believe he would. I believe he would stop at nothing, that man—not even at that, old as I am. I believe he is evil through and through. He has made it a law, you see—those two told me that he has made it a law: anyone who knows who any of the Loblollies are, must die. And nothing is to stand in the way of that law—of any of his laws."

The thin sensitive face of the old man had grown a little paler. He swept his hand nervously through his long white hair.

"These two you saw, sir," asked Harry, "—were they village men?—Lytchett men?"

"Perhaps I should say no more, Harry," the old man said quietly. "You must not ask me any more. All I know is that from that day forward, someone leaves a little keg for me most Moonshine nights at the door. I wish sometimes that they would not—lest Blackadder should see them and guess, perhaps—or try to find out from them why they leave me the gift. But yet, I cannot deny that—well, it is better brandy than I can buy, and I have always liked good brandy, lads! . . ."

He smiled a little, and some of his apprehension went away from him.

"Come," he said, "—we mustn't be gloomy like this —it's not what you came for, surely. We have very little time this evening—if the Moonshiners are to be out you must go early, lads; and so we shall have our refreshments immediately, and then perhaps just a little music—for half an hour or so."

He rose and went to the cupboard in the corner where he kept the shortcake and ale with which he usually regaled the boys on their visits. A poker was already heating in the fire, and by the hob was a bowl of sugar and some grated nutmeg. His movements always slow and deliberate but full of a gentle grace, he poured a jug of the weak ale and set it down on the hearth. Then he took the poker from the coals, and, after holding it close to his face for a moment to test its heat, plunged it into the tankard. There was a hiss and a little burst of steam as he held it steady for a moment in the liquid. Then he set it down, took up the jug and poured out two tankards of the warm brew, and sprinkled the sugar and nutmeg into them.

"There, lads. And if you will give me a moment to fetch a little of that very Moonshine we have been talking of for myself, we shall toast to—to what?"

"The downfall of Blackadder," said Tom. "And may he never learn anything of the story you have told us."

"Agreed—agreed, Tom. The downfall of Blackadder, and an end to all his wickedness! "

He raised the glass he had poured for himself, and so they drank. And as the warm sweet mixture went through his veins, Tom had a sudden vision of the little black keg that he and Harry had seen in the cove that afternoon—and in spite of what he knew of Blackadder, in spite of what the old man had told them of his terrible law of death, there grew stronger in him at that very instant the resolution that he had formed as he had walked home with Philadelphia from Harry's house. He found himself half-wishing already that their visit to Mr. Abershaw was over, so that he could tell Harry what was in his mind.

And so they sat quietly together by the fire, and after a moment or two Mr. Abershaw took up his flute and played to them. But somehow, that evening, there was a restlessness in all three of them, and the visit was not so successful as such occasions usually were. Outside, after the long and unusual heat of the day—that day of all days, the 18th of May 1803—outside there was a heavy oppressiveness in the air—a hint of thunder. Already, as Tom had walked across the sand-dunes with Phil, great clouds had been gathering, overcasting the sky; and when he had met Harry outside Mr. Abershaw's house, the air had been still and sinister, with the potent scent of forthcoming storm in it.

The old man set down the flute at last and sighed. He stayed for a moment quietly, looking into the glowing fire.

"Troubled times," he murmured, half to himself. "Ah, troubled times! There will be war again—at any moment there must be war, if it has not broken even already, perhaps. The flower of our country will go out to die. Perhaps it will go on for long enough for you to have to go too, lads—who knows? There will be death and bloodshed and a deal of heartache before all is over. And all for what?—the ambition of one man to rule all the world, the dream of one nation to stand above all other nations. And all the time what we really need—what each one of us really wants in his heart—is something as quiet and simple as that little tune I played to Papa Haydn once: a moment of comfort before a fire and four walls to live in at peace with all men, always. . . ."

And he raised the flute to his lips again and played the air delicately and with infinite feeling. It mingled strangely with the first far-off rumble of the thunder from across the sea, and for a moment he hesitated at the turn of a phrase, his eyes dimmed over and with even a hint of tears in them.

And it was then, in that strange moment, as he confessed long afterwards, that the resolution crystallised at last in Tom Cathro and he determined on a course of action that was to carry him and Harry de Rohan through adventures unimaginable, through suffering and hardship and nightmare to the very point of death itself. . . .

When they were outside he outlined his scheme to Harry.

"You see," he said, "we know where the Loblollies land on Moonshine nights—or at least we think we do. If we could be sure—if we once knew for certain, and had some idea of who they were—even of who Blackadder is—there might be some way to end the whole thing."

"What do you mean, Tom? How could we?"

"Look, Harry—here is a whole village frightened to very death by one man whom nobody even knows. You know as well as I do that when the sign goes up that it's to be a Moonshine night, not one soul in the whole of Lytchett dares to put his face outside his house. And all for what?—why?—*why?*"

"Smuggling—everyone knows that. Smuggling—except on a bigger scale than usual."

"We all believe there's something more than simple smuggling in it. Nobody minds smuggling—there's always been smuggling in this part of the country. There's not a fisherman on the whole south coast but has helped to get Moonshine in—my own father used to run with the smugglers when he was young—he told me himself before he died. But in the old days it was never like this—this man Blackadder has organised it in a new kind of way—it's something different altogether. And it must be stopped—it must."

"How can it be stopped, Tom? It's gone too far by this time—the coastguards are supposed to be under Blackadder's thumb as much as everybody else—otherwise how is it that there are no raids on Moonshine nights?"

"The real trouble is there aren't enough coastguards —that's probably why Blackadder came into this district in the first place. All the coastguards have been drawn along to other parts of the coast—along to Sussex and Kent—so that they can act as lookouts if war does break and Napoleon tries to invade us. There are only a handful of them left here—and maybe they have been bribed, I don't know—maybe they're only terrified of Blackadder, the same as everybody else is."

"What *could* we do then?"

"Go elsewhere. My mother told me this morning that there's some of the Press Gang down at the Inn—they arrived yesterday—a naval Lieutenant and half-a-dozen men. They've started already pressing men for Southampton and Portsmouth—lest the war does start. And there's Squire Westwood too—even if some of the authorities are being bribed, I know in my bones that the Squire isn't. Well, then—by the time war is declared, smuggling isn't simple smuggling any longer—it's trading with the enemy—it's treason. I'm not sure it isn't treason already, even, with the war so close. And at the very smell of treason Squire Westwood will drop everything and attack—you know how patriotic he is. He'll get troops from Dorchester or Poole—and the Naval Officer with the Press Gang will help him too. And we could ambush Blackadder one night in the cove and get him that way."

"If we can be certain that it is the cove he lands at."

"We can *make* certain! This very night—if you are ready to take the risk, Harry."

The young Frenchman stopped in his tracks and

whistled softly. In the darkness Tom saw his white, suddenly tense face turned towards him.

"Tom—you mean——"

"I mean that you and I will go down to the cove to-night, Harry—this very night—by ourselves. We can hide somewhere—we can watch the whole thing. We can find out what Blackadder looks like, and then we can be ready to tell the Squire everything to-morrow."

In the darkness Harry's voice sounded doubtful.

"And yet, Tom—suppose—suppose something goes wrong——"

"Nothing need go wrong—why should it? Harry, don't you see we must do it? As long as Blackadder is at large no one in this whole village is safe. You and I aren't safe—Phil isn't. Suppose your grandfather went out one Moonshine night—suppose he happened to run across the Loblollies at work. He would be killed on the spot. . . . You saw that old man we were with to-night—whom we both like so much—Mr. Abershaw. You saw how frightened he was. Suppose Blackadder finds out why those two men leave him a keg of brandy every Moonshine night? No, Harry— it was while Mr. Abershaw was telling us all that to-night that I saw that you and I would *have* to do something. I had half-decided earlier, when I was walking home with Phil—but I grew absolutely cer-tain when I learned that Mr. Abershaw was in danger —real danger."

They were standing now before the gate of Harry's house, and for a long moment they faced each other, their faces set and strained in the moonlight that struggled through the massing storm clouds. After his long mounting speech Tom was silent, his heart beating strongly in his breast. And, at the end, when he spoke again, it was suddenly more quietly and seriously:

"Harry, we must do it—we must find out if it is the cove Blackadder lands at. There's more in it all than anything I've said. We all have the impression that Blackadder isn't only a smuggler—you know we have. There's something behind all this that's bigger and wickeder than bringing simple contraband into the country. Otherwise why should there be all this secrecy?—why should Blackadder be afraid for anyone to see him? There have been smugglers before and everyone has known who they were—it hasn't mattered at all. This is something deeper—this is something evil, Harry—really evil. And that's another reason why I must go to-night—even if you won't come with me. I must find out what Blackadder really looks like and what he really does—I must!"

Again for a long moment there was silence between them. In the house beyond the dark garden they could see the flickering of a light from room to room, and at one of the downstairs windows the tall thin shadow of the Chevalier de Rohan appeared, seeming to peer out anxiously into the night—looking for his grandson.

"I will come with you, Tom," said Harry softly—almost inaudibly. He reached out his hand and touched his friend's arm. "You're right—of course you're right. We must find out—and we must find out together."

And so they stayed for a moment longer, making whispered plans; and then Harry turned and ran into the house and Tom went hurrying himself along the village street to his mother's cottage; and his heart was singing in the prospect of action.

CHAPTER FIVE

ON THE BEACH

"... *I have seen much, I have done much; I have adventured in foreign lands and upon the high seas; I have been within a sight of death and wrestled with fear itself. But in all my long days of travel and travail I have known no such terror as gripped me in the heart long ago—long ago when I was a boy; and I encountered for the first time, face to face, the monstrous figure we knew as Blackadder. . . ."*

AND NOW it was near the end of that long strange day which was the start of all the adventure and which I have tried to reconstruct from the various fragments of writing which Tom Cathro and Harry de Rohan left behind them when they died long ago. Some episodes in the story—those dealing with the main part of the adventure—were worked out in full, and those will be presented in due course. But this first part was only sketched imperfectly, and so it has been my task, as editor, to try to re-create, however inadequately, the happenings of that long bright day of May in 1803. This prelude of mine, however, begins to move towards its end; and so, if you will bear with me a little longer, I shall gather together the threads that remain, and so pass you over for a space to those other storytellers more qualified than I to take the adventure further along its course.

It was almost ten o'clock that night, and Tom and Harry together had taken up their position in the cove —in the shadow of that very boulder behind which Philadelphia had hidden earlier. At half-past nine they had met, as by their arrangement. Each had ostensibly gone to bed—and had gone early, as was the accepted custom for young folk in Lytchett on a Moonshine night. But each had lain awake for a long chill hour; and at last, at the appointed moment, had crept to dress. Tom had lowered himself to the meadow behind his mother's cottage from his bedroom window—it was a short drop from the sill, no more than a few feet. He had stood for a moment in the silence close to the very spot where once he had seen the King of Smugglers himself—the man whose identity he was determined to learn—or at least whose face he was determined to see clearly at last, so that he could betray him. Then he had scurried forward to the little copse at the side of Harry's house where the two had agreed to meet.

He found Harry waiting for him, pale and a little breathless. For him, it had been a little more difficult to get out of the house. His grandfather had not gone to bed himself until close on a quarter-past-nine—and Harry knew that it was the old man's custom to look in at his grandson's room to see that all was well with him before he retired. If he had stayed up beyond nine-thirty it would have been impossible for Harry to have left the house. When the Chevalier did look in, the candle held high in his hand, the boy pretended to sleep. He heard the old man's quiet sigh, his murmured blessing; and followed his footsteps along the corridor to his own room—listened to the far-off closing of the Chevalier's bedroom door—before he ventured to stir. The drop from his window was too high to be tackled in safety, and so he had to creep along the corridor and down the inner stairs to the landing below, where it was possible for him to prise open a window and so reach the ground by way of the sloping roof of a little outhouse.

In silence, they made their way stealthily from the little copse to the shore, avoiding the main pathway, cutting across fields and heading thus for the cliff-top. They shivered, not from the cold, for the air that night was still oppressive, the thunder rumbling distantly, but from the close excitement of what they were doing. At one point, as they went, great heavy drops of rain began to fall—slowly, as it seemed, as in a nightmare, rustling and splashing on the leaves and grasses.

The tide was in as they knew, and so there was no hope of approaching the cove by the shore path; it was a matter of descending the rough stepway cut into the rocks which they knew the smugglers themselves would be using. As they reached the top of the cliffs they held back in the shelter of some bushes lest they were too late in their timing, and some of the smugglers had already assembled. But all was quiet; and at a darker moment they stealthily moved forward again and clambered down the path, hugging the wall of rock as they went.

And now at last they were in position, waiting, lying close together, aware of the dampness of the sand through their clothes and with the pungent night-smell of the sea in their nostrils.

It was dark in the extreme; only occasionally did the great storm clouds overhead drift apart for a moment and the moonlight struggle through. They grew cramped in their constrained positions, and, as they reckoned, it was long past ten o'clock itself. But still nothing happened—they heard no sound beyond the low lap and moan of the sea before them.

They shifted position slightly, Tom crouching on his knees for a moment to relieve the cramp he was beginning to suffer. Harry buried his face in his hands and coughed, as quietly as he could, as the sea-air caught him at the throat. And at that moment he felt Tom grip him in the arm, and heard his whispered voice close up to his ear.

"We were right, Harry—oh, we were right! Look there!"

He followed the dim shape of his friend's pointing arm, and low down on the sea's surface, at a point beyond the last of the outjutting rocks of the Teeth, he saw the sudden dim glimmer of a light.

Simultaneously there came the stealthy sounds of footsteps on the rock path behind them—but not many footsteps, no more than four or five pairs, as they reckoned. They crunched forward on the sand and shingle, and a moment later a little group of shadowy figures passed close to the boulder and moved towards the left-hand shoulder of the cove itself.

They felt that they hardly dared to breathe—they trembled violently as they pressed close together, peering forward. Again from their vantage point they saw the glim of the light at sea—closer now, much closer. And it was answered by the glow of a dark lantern from the little group on the shore—and suddenly, cutting through the oppressive silence there was the low repeated call of an owl.

Then silence again—and darkness—thick darkness, as a cloud that was heavier than the others obscured the moon. They waited—they waited. . . .

At last the light again—almost inshore—by one of the needle rocks of the Teeth; and a scraping of bulkhead planks and a muttering of voices.

"One boat," whispered Tom—no more than a breath in Harry's ear. "Only one! And no more than four of them on the shore there. . . . What does it mean, Harry? The cove should be full of them if we were right—there should be a whole fleet out there, not only one boat . . . ."

Harry did not answer. He gripped Tom's arm tightly and pointed; and as the cloud passed they could make out something of the group to their left. The boat, they saw, was no more than a gig, and it had been anchored by a painter to one of the inner needle-rocks. A man was wading to the shore, towards the figures standing closely huddled at the water-line. And on his shoulder was what seemed to be a large flat box.

As he neared the beach he stumbled a little and one of the watching men sprang forward to help him. They heard the words, "Gently, gently!" borne suddenly clearly to them on the still air. And they saw one figure, standing a little apart from the others, his hand upraised—a figure unbelievably tall in the dim light, his back to them, but, to Tom at least, his whole thin evil shape a memory.

"Blackadder," he whispered. "He is there!—he is there himself! . . ."

An instant later he was lying tense again, holding his breath; for two of the men were moving up the beach towards them, carrying the box.

They set it down, moving with a strange gentleness as it seemed; and from where the boys lay the box was no more than a few yards distant. Then the men returned to the water-line, and, as the boys followed them in their movement with their eyes, it was to see that another similar box was being carried ashore by the second man from the boat.

Again the two men of the shore party carried the box up the beach and laid it down with the other, and once more they returned to where their companions waited. But this time they stayed with the others, and it was clear from the way in which all the figures drew together in one dark huddled shape in the gloom that some conference between them was taking place.

"Two boxes," whispered Tom. "Only the two. . . ."

He lay puzzling the whole matter deeply. He had expected, from all that he knew of the Moonshiners, from all he suspected of the size and purpose of Blackadder's organisation, that the cove that night would have been full of boats and men—that for many hours a stealthy unloading of contraband would have gone forward. Instead, he and Harry had seen an assembly of no more than half-a-dozen men—Blackadder and five others, the three who had approached with him down the cliff path and the two from the boat. And instead of the heaped kegs and boxes he had expected to see mounting up on the shore before them, there were two small boxes only—and not even boxes, as he saw now, in a sudden gleam of the moonlight: baskets—flat oblong baskets. . . .

And even as he looked at them there seemed to come from them a low throaty murmur—from the baskets themselves. He stared incredulously and strained his ears; and again the soft whisper was repeated—a low gentle *purring* as it seemed, hollow and indistinct.

Then suddenly his attention was diverted to the group at the water-line. He saw that two of the men were wading out once more to the boat, the others standing back and separating from them. He heard the lapping of the wavelets against the side of the gig as the men embarked in her, and a moment later, to his further astonishment, there was the scrape of an oar against the rock, the flash of its blade in the moonlight, and the boat was pushing out to sea again, as silently and mysteriously as it had come.

Simultaneously the group on the shore moved across the shingle—and, as they did so, a great and terrible light broke upon him. He knew, he suddenly knew, what was concealed in the baskets before him—he had recognised the soft throaty cooing, which had continued throughout all the movement further down the beach. And he heard something else too—something which caused his whole world to topple. The tall figure advancing from the water-line before all the others—the tall dark shape of Blackadder himself—was whistling softly. And the air he whistled was the air of a little Serenade of Haydn which he had heard barely three hours before in the warm snug room of Mr. Abershaw's cottage.

He drew his breath in a sharp terrified gasp that cut through the still air like a knife. The whistling stopped on the instant. There was a long deadly silence—and far off, across the sea, the menacing rumble of the thunder. . . .

He looked up. The moon was clear. Blackadder had stopped no more than a pace or two away from them where they crouched. He was perfectly still and his shadow fell towards them across the silvered sand—fell over them, their two faces mere white patches in its depths.

And Blackadder held in his hand, pointing straight towards them, a small black round-eyed pistol. And the silence was full of the soft chill sound of his laughter.

"My young friends!" he said quietly, in a voice they knew—but a voice which had an edge to it that they had never heard before. "My young friends, come to spy on me! And all my secret known at last, I think!..."

And the face the boys looked up at in the moonlight was the face they had looked at too a bare three hours earlier—but now it was thinned and pale and barely recognisable to them. The hair which fell down on each side of it was no longer white but jet black; the face itself was no longer old and gentle, but young and sardonic and full of an unutterable sense of evil. But it was still the face they had known as the face of Mr. Abershaw.

And hoarsely, unrecognisably in that moment of sheer terror, Tom heard his own voice speaking—and the distorted, unreal tones of it mingled with the impassive cooing of the pigeons that lay in the baskets before them.

"You're a spy—a spy! Blackadder—you—you! And a spy!"

"As you say, my young friend—a spy. Why not? It can be an honourable profession—depending upon which side you regard it from. The pity is that you will not live long enough to benefit in any way from the knowledge you have so indiscreetly gained—nor will your country gain from it. Indeed, in a sense, it would be too late in any case for either of you to gain from it—all too late, my poor young friend!"

"What do you mean? At least if I am to die I have the right to know what you mean before I do!"

"Certainly—most certainly. It will take the veriest moment. . . ." He nodded for an instant towards the two baskets on the sand between them. "You have surmised, I think, that being a spy I have my methods of gaining important information. These doves of mine—which all of you thought so harmless in Mr. Abershaw's charming cotes—these little *messengers*, shall I say, come in to me from every quarter bearing news—and have done so for many months. Some few of them came in a little earlier this evening—indeed, not long after you left me at the end of our delightful little musical session. They brought me great news, my young friend—news which is already known all over England, but which has not yet penetrated to this particular small corner of it in the normal way. Oh, they brought me news which you are most certainly entitled to hear, I think!"

He paused; and it was as if for an instant even his tall figure grew taller, and his face was upthrown and shone white and fanatical in the gleam of the moonshine.

"This day is the eighteenth day of May in this year of eighteen hundred and three. Mark it well, my friend—let it burn in your heart—remember it always! On this day England again declared war against my beloved France. The Peace of Amiens is at an end. Your country and mine, Mr. Cathro, are at war— implacably at war! And this time there will be no peace—until it be the peace of death for one or other of us!"

PART TWO

"*BLOW, WINDS, AND CRACK YOUR CHEEKS!*"

Being a continuation of the story of BLACK-ADDER from the point of the capture on Lytchett beach, recollected and written in his mature age

by
Admiral Sir Thomas Cathro

I MARVEL now, looking back, that we were not killed upon the spot. Or rather I should say that I marvelled *then*; for in due course we learned something of the troubled history of the Spy Blackadder, and were illuminated in some of the designs he had formed; and so it was a mystery no longer. But at the time it was.

I shall propose at some other moment to complete the earlier part of our tale: how when I was fourteen I made, with my friend Harry de Rohan (now the distinguished head of the great house of Rowan and Sons, Wine Merchants, and rightful Chevalier de Rohan-Soubise), the terrible discovery that the man we had taken to be the gentle Mr. Abershaw, and our friend, was indeed the notorious Blackadder. Moreover, that the whole organisation which went by the name of the Loblolly Boys, and which we had taken to be but a smuggling game upon the grand scale, was the cloak for the more desperate matter of spying.

It would be as well, perhaps, at this point, before proceeding with our further adventures after our capture by Blackadder on the beach, to sketch something of the man's activities in his dual role, as we later were able to piece them together from what he himself told us and from what we learned from other members of his gang—notably the Frenchman Kabal and the renegade Scot, Habbakuk McGuffie.

The Life of a Spy

It seems, then, telling it as briefly as may be, that the man Blackadder was of mixed stock: his father an Anglo-Scot, his mother a Frenchwoman. He was brought up in his early times in London, but from the age of fifteen onwards, when his father died, he was conveyed to live in France.

He was, at the time when we first encountered him, some thirty-five years old. Thus, he had been in his youth an active participant in the great Revolution in France. He was, it seems, most violently imbued indeed with revolutionary notions; was an associate of such extremists as Marat and Robespierre; and was a fanatical informer and assassin of the aristocrats at the time of the Reign of Terror.

The Revolution over, Blackadder threw himself furiously into the first war between England and France. For some reason which we have never discovered he was consumed by a fearful and continuous hatred against our country—he had associated himself body and soul with his mother's people. He campaigned with Bonaparte in Italy, was present at the Battle of the Nile (at which, as all the world knows, our great Admiral Nelson so distinguished himself), and fought at Marengo.

But already he was showing signs, as it seems, that his true vocation lay not in soldiering, but in spying. There was that in his twisted nature—imbued as it was (as we had much evidence hereafter in confirmation) with an essence of pure evil—which responded to the subtleties and perversities of that dangerous, ignoble game. So it was that with the signing of the uneasy Peace of Amiens, between France and England, in 1802, he came truly into his own.

All the world knew that the Peace was unlikely to last—how could it indeed, in the face of the over-weening ambition of Bonaparte, whose avowed aim from the moment he was created First Consul of France in 1799, was to rule the whole great globe? The peace, indeed, was designed as no more than a breathing space: both sides continued to prepare, to build up their resources against the occasion of a fresh outbreak of hostilities.

Because of his English ancestry, and his consequent full command of the language, the man Simon Blackadder was sent to England for the purpose of building an organisation which would supply our restless enemy across the Channel with information concerning all our plans and preparations.

The details of the creation of the Spy Ring are too complex to go into here: it will suffice to say that before he had been in the country many months, Blackadder had established agents in every English port and barrack town. He was an adept at disguise, and to conceal himself and his activites, he adopted the role of an elderly music-master by the name of Abershaw. This he contrived very simply by wearing a white wig and by lining his face, by walking with a stoop, assuming an attitude of gentle frailty. I can testify, as can my friend Harry Rowan (none better!), to the total success of his device.

As Abershaw, then, he set up his headquarters in a house in Soho in London; and it rapidly became the centre of a far-flung and efficient spy-ring which, throughout the early days of the Peace, caused much trouble to our own Secret Police. No one suspected the genial old music-master, who played the flute so admirably (it was a paradox in this man's evil character that he genuinely loved music), who conducted such pleasant musical soirées, who claimed, with the utmost conviction, to have been a personal friend of such masters as Haydn, Salomon, and even Beethoven.

But the pose had its difficulties. He found certain trouble in communicating to France itself, from London, the information gathered by the Ring. Moreover, slight suspicion was beginning to be centred upon the lodgings in Soho where he flourished. And so it was, first to perfect his system of communication, and second, to escape from the prying eyes of our Service, that he conceived his master-stroke.

From his study of our defences along the south coast, he knew that certain tracts of country were not so well covered as others. All through the period of of the Peace, we were convinced in England that when war did break again it would take the form of an attempt at invasion by Bonaparte. We consequently assembled many of our defence forces along those parts of the coast where such an invasion might reasonably be expected to be launched—near Dover, along the southern coasts of Kent and Sussex. To provide us adequately with lookouts along these shores, we drew away from other parts of the coast, less dangerous, whole bodies of coastguards; and this meant, naturally, that such districts—such isolated small districts as our own territory in South Dorset, between Poole and Swanage, were virtually unmanned.

Into our village of Lytchett, then, came Spy Blackadder; and I will disclose no secret before its time if I merely say at this stage that by something of a coincidence he was serving yet another of his nefarious ends by so doing—on this occasion a private one. However, of this more anon; meanwhile to proceed with the more immediate matter.

For many years the fishermen in our part of the country had been engaged—illicitly, of course, but still innocently—in smuggling activities across the Channel: bringing in contraband materials such as brandy, wines, tobaccos and laces—the Moonshine, as it was called, from the fact that it was mainly shipped in in secret moonlight voyages. This activity had been curtailed to an extent by the war between the two countries; but with the coming of the Peace it broke out again in full flower.

Now, our smugglers had only operated in small isolated groups before; but Blackadder saw that by gathering them altogether in one central organisation, he could not only *provide himself with an easy method of getting information back and forth across the Channel* but (no mean consideration to such a man as this!) enrich himself considerably in the process.

Thus he acted, then. As Mr. Abershaw, retired

music-master from London, he delighted us all by day; as Blackadder—the dreaded Blackadder—he terrorised our countryside by night. By dint of threats, of acts of murder—even, as we discovered, on one or two occasions of the most brutal torture—he drew together into one band all the smugglers near our village. Those who would not join him were forced to give up the game altogether, or were destroyed as a warning to others. He deliberately traded upon the menace of his name—his own name. No one knew who he was—for the most part the organisation was so built, indeed, that each man in it knew only the others in the little group with whom he particularly worked. Thus, there were those who sailed the little boats to and fro across the sea; there were those who merely unloaded the Moonshine as it landed; there were those who conveyed it from the beaches to the cities and there disposed of it: and thereafter the money was divided down all the line, and instead of flourishing as free-traders in their own right, the smuggling men of Lytchett became mere wage-earners, in the thrall of the one mastermind who issued all the orders and laid all the plans. He found it easy, of course, because of his secret connection with France, to build an organisation upon the other side which supplied the Moonshiners with the contraband material itself; and, because of the fact that those few coastguards who did remain in our district were either bribed or completely terrorised, he was able to continue his operations with hardly any interference.

To make sure that everything was still kept secret

(since he was engaged in spying as well as smuggling), he contrived things so that on Moonshine nights a sign was displayed in the village which acted as a warning to all our people to remain hidden—the sign of a freshly-killed adder (trading again upon the sinister ring of his own name) nailed on a board. Anyone innocently trespassing upon his activities on such Moonshine nights was instantly murdered; and in this way it came about that the name of Blackadder was a menace and a terror to our whole village. Who he was himself, no one knew. Occasionally the members of the Band—Loblollies, as they were called, from the old cant name for the smuggling fraternity—glimpsed him at a distance, but all they saw on these occasions was a tall thin figure swathed in black—sufficient to make them realise that there was indeed such a man as Blackadder.

And all the time, as the Moonshine trade went on, the men who crossed the Channel to and fro were, in addition to contraband, innocently carrying messages to enemy agents—arming Napoleon with information of the utmost danger to the safety of our beloved country!

And Blackadder went further. He found that there were occasions when it was necessary for messages to be passed more quickly than they could be carried by boats on the occasional Moonshine nights. In his role of Abershaw he had struck upon the innocent idea of keeping pigeons; what more natural than that for a gentle elderly man such as he represented himself to be? But pigeons, as he realised, were more than pets

—from time immemorial homing pigeons had been used by man for carrying messages. Therefore, he now began an ingenious development of the Moonshine notion.

Among the contraband material smuggled in were occasional baskets of homing pigeons. These had been trained, of course, to home to a depot somewhere in France. Thus, if one of his agents in London or Portsmouth sent him a vital message, it was only necessary for him to enclose it in a little cylinder attached to one of the legs of a French-homing pigeon, and to send it literally flying across the sea.

Similarly, baskets of pigeons trained to fly to his cotes in Lytchett were conveyed to France, and could be used to send messages from his colleagues there to him. And finally, other pigeons were conveyed to his agents in London and other cities, so that at any moment information could be hurried to and fro. . . .

And this was the man who confronted us that night —that night of May 18 in the year 1803, when war again broke out between France and England. This was the man who stayed silent before us in the moonlight, his pistol aimed and steady at our heads!

A Knock at the Door

We expected death—what else could we expect, in view of all we had ever heard of Blackadder? And for a moment it seemed indeed that he would murder us there upon the spot. But suddenly, as he confronted us there was a movement from one of the men beside him—a lank and torpid creature, near as tall as he was himself. This man moved forward and touched Blackadder on the arm.

"What is it, Kabal?" the Spy snarled, making impatiently to shake off the other's arm. But the man Kabal had leaned close up to him, and now whispered something in his ear.

Blackadder started; and suddenly nodded, with a quick malignant glance at Harry. Then he beckoned to one of the other figures beside him, this one smaller, rotund, with a blank ruddy face and straggled sandy hair.

"Gag them—bind their arms," he said abruptly. And added, with a sudden angry gesture of the pistol: "Hurry, man—hurry! There's devilish little time to waste—we're held back long enough already!"

The round man came forward and jerked me to my feet, the while Kabal did likewise for Harry. He dragged a foul-smelling rag from his cloak-pocket and wrenched it crudely across my mouth, pulling it tight till I felt my blood pound. As he worked in this way, and at tying my hands behind me with a thin cord, he muttered half to himself:

"There, laddie—there ye are, sir! Ye'll no get oot o' that in a hurry. I was aye good at knots. There! Man, it's a beauty that yin! It's a real reef—nane o' yer granny knots for me! I mind fine my auld mither telling me——"

"Hold your tongue, McGuffie," hissed Blackadder.

"The devil take your endless babbling! Are they ready?"

"The very picture of a pair of trussit cockerels, yer honour. I never did a better job."

"Bring them on, then—after me. Kabal, see to de Rohan—hold them—hold them both. If they get away from you you're answerable to me."

He strode forward and the two men jostled Harry and me after him. The man McGuffie had me firmly in his grasp at the shoulder—gripped till I was near fainting from the sharp bite of his fingers in my bone. We staggered on the shingle as best as we could, out of balance with our hands tied, and were half-pushed, half-dragged up the cliff-path. Once I stumbled and fell against the ragged wall—and felt a stab of pain at my temple as the rock scraped me, and a smear of blood blinded over my eye.

"Steady, steady," said the man behind me. "Ye'll hurt yoursel, laddie!—watch what wey ye're goin! . . ."

And his voice was full of a genuine homely concern, it seemed!—which was, however, belied by the sudden increase in his grip at my shoulder.

When we reached the top, and scrambled helplessly over the edge, it was to see Blackadder's grim tall shape striding out across the fields at full pace in the direction of the village. He moved perfectly openly—indeed arrogantly; and it crossed my mind even then that it was an index to the full power he felt he had over all our people. He had so terrorised them that he could move freely wherever he wished on Moonshine nights, with no thought of possible danger.

My eyes seemed starting out of my head by the time we reached the cottage where we had been accustomed to spending so much time with our friend Abershaw. My blood pounded through my ears from the pressure of the gag and the exertion of our hurried forced journey. My head was splitting—I felt faint and ready to drop.

We were thrust forward through the little corridor and into the very room we had visited earlier—where we had heard the little air of Haydn which, as he rapidly pulled the shutters across, Blackadder was whistling even now between his teeth. Our captors thrust us forward into two chairs as Blackadder lit a second lantern from the one which burned low already in the room.

"Aye, aye," said McGuffie. "Well, here ye are, laddies—and it'll be a while ere ye take to monkeying aboot on beaches again, I'm thinking. Ye're a bonny pair, I must say, and you just bairns. Ye should have kent better than to try to have a keek at the Maister here."

"Before heaven, McGuffie, I'll have that tongue of yours out of your head before we're done to-night! Why the deuce must you talk, man?"

"It's just a failing, yer honour—just an auld failing! It's been a bane to me all my days. It was the same when I was a bairn myself. My auld mither was fair deeved wi' it times—oh, sir, I've had many a skelpit lug for no haudin my wheesht——"

"Hold your tongue!"

For an instant the face before us twisted in an

insane rage. The black cloak swung back with a sudden gesture and he half drew the sabre we now saw swinging at his waist. McGuffie, barely abashed, it seemed, fell silent with a muttered:

"A' right, a' right, sir! I can tak' a hint as well as the next man, I'm sure! "

I glanced across at my friend Harry. His face was deadly white above the gag, his eyes strained in pain. Beyond him was the music stand round which we had sat barely three hours before—and resting on it innocently the flute which Abershaw so often had played to us. And a great horror and loathing was in me for the evil being before us. In the new lamplight we were seeing him clearly for the first time; and the face, which had been so old and gentle before, now seemed a grotesque and horrible caricature in its thin, contorted wickedness.

At this moment the third of Blackadder's companions came into the room. He was a gross, low-stooped fellow, immensely strong, to judge from his girth and breadth of shoulder. His face was coarse and unshaven, the eyes pig-like, the brow a mere line below the mat of his hair. We had been aware of this fellow following behind us on the journey from the beach, carrying single-handed on his shoulder the two pigeon baskets.

"All stowed, Rush? " Blackadder asked, with a glance at him.

"All stowed, master. In the loft—I set 'em down just as they were."

"Good—good. There are some messages that must

be sent by them. Kabal, have you the papers that came in earlier? "

The tall saturnine figure of the man who was plainly his chief lieutenant advanced towards him, holding out an envelope, and Blackadder snatched it and scanned through the thin rice-paper notes it contained—notes plainly flown to him, to judge from the way they were folded, in the little cylinders attached to the legs of the pigeons.

Now and again, as he read, he muttered closely to himself; then, with another sudden gesture, he swept forward out of the room again, signalling to Kabal to follow him.

The moment he was gone the other two seemed immediately to grow easier in manner. The fellow called Rush strode over to the cupboard where, as we knew, the ale and other drinks were kept, and took out a flagon of brandy.

"Man, man, a great idea!" said the irrepressible McGuffie. "I'm sure the Maister will never mind if we just wet our whistles with a wee taste of the stuff itsel'. Ye'll just pass me the bottle when ye've done with it, Billy."

Rush grunted and handed over the bottle. He had poured himself a substantial noggin from it and now tossed it back in one gulp. He shook his bull-head stupidly for a moment and then flopped down in a low chair, which groaned and tottered beneath his sudden weight.

"Ye'll no' mind Billy, lads," said McGuffie pleasantly —in the tone of a simple social conversation. "He's no' that bright—his auld nannie must have drapped him on that ba'-heid o' his when he was a bairn. Like as no' he'll be dozin' off to sleep in a two-three minutes —Billy thinks o' nothing but his sleep."

He had seated himself jovially before us, the bottle clasped lovingly in his hands—which, as I saw, were unexpectedly slender in so round a man. But that they were strong enough I had every reason to recollect, from the pain which still throbbed in my shoulder.

"I'm thinking maybe the pair o' ye could do wi' a wee stretch," went on McGuffie genially. "It cannae be a' that comfortable for ye the way ye are. Well, well, we'll just see what we can do—the Maister'll maybe no mind if I just ease yer arms a wee and loosen they gags a bit. Mind, ye're no' tae try any fancy stuff if I do loose ye up a shade! If there's the least wee peep from ye I'll just hae to tickle ye up a bit wi' my bit whinger here."

And, smiling pleasantly, he drew out from his belt a long, thin, evil-looking weapon—a short sword rather than a knife—and set it on a small table close to his hand. Then he advanced towards us and loosened the ropes at our wrists, and the knots in the gags at the back of our heads.

The relief was immense—I could have cried out in the joy of it. But McGuffie had settled himself—still with his friendly smile, but with the long knife laid across his knee; and so I did nothing but wriggle slightly to ease the circulation in my arms.

"Hech, lads, it's a life, it's a life!" went on McGuffie. "Here we are, the four o' us, and a queerer-like crew ye couldnae find in a day's march. Twa interferin' laddies and a pair o' rogues like Billy and me, eh? What wey did ye want to nose in like that on the Maister's business, eh? It's a' right—ye can speak if ye like—the gags are loose enough for that now. It's just ye've no' tae try any funny stuff, ye ken."

"We did what should have been done long ago," I said shortly. "We tried to find out who Blackadder was, so that we could put an end to all his wickedness."

"Well, well. Is that so, then! Wickedness, is it? Well, maybe it is, maybe it is! Ye'll be meaning this spying dodge we've been up to for a while?"

"We didn't know it was spying. It was bad enough when it was terrorising all the country the way he's been doing—that's what we wanted to stop. But now that we do know it's spying there's all the more reason."

"Ach, well! It's just a question of the way ye look at it. See me, now—an honest Scotsman frae Lanark. Ye'll be thinking it's a queer-like thing for me to be wrapped up in—and I'll no' deny but there have been whiles when I've thocht that that auld mither o' mine would be gey sair-hearted to see her laddie in this prank. But ye see, when I met the Maister a while back, he fair swept me off my feet. Hech, yon fellow can talk!—ye should hear him! He can talk and talk! He blames me for the blethering whiles, but when he gets going himsel' I'm no in it! And ye see, when I got into a bit trouble wi' the press gang boys—after I'd deserted from the navy, that is—and that was after I had the flogging for insulting a superior officer, ye see—and that was after I'd tellt him—well, never mind what I tellt him! Anyway, I wasnae feeling all that pleased wi' His Majesty's Navy, ye'll understand, or His Majesty himsel' for that matter, and when the Maister ups and says he'd pay me well for a bit harmless help—well, what did I care if it was maybe going a bit contrary to what my auld mither had taught me? I'm sure there's no' much difference between working for the King or working for Boney—and if ye think that Boney's sure to win, the wey the Maister does, and so if ye know what side your bread is buttered on, so to say. . . . well, when it came to the bit, I just said to myself, Habbie McGuffie, says I, ye'd better just do what the Maister says and help Boney *instead* o' the King, and if your auld mither ever *does* get to hear of it, and her maybe still alive for all I ken back in Lanark there——"

There seemed indeed no reason why this endless tirade of his should ever stop. But at this moment, sheering through the long monotonous drone of his Scottish voice, there came a sudden sharp rapping at the door; and McGuffie stopped full in mid sentence and snatched up in readiness the long kife that lay across his knee and which he had been fondling all the time he talked—as Abershaw earlier, in that very room, had fondled the flute . . . .

A Wounded Man

There was a moment, as I recollect it now, looking back across the years, of utter icy silence. McGuffie held up his long evil-looking knife; across from him, slumped stupidly in the low chair, was Rush, his jaw sagged open a little, his small pig eyes staring. And at the doorway of the room, as I could see by turning my head a little, stood Kabal, who had been on the point of entering, as it seemed, at the moment of the knock, with Blackadder's own white face beyond his shoulder.

So we stayed—and I believe I would have cried out, as Harry too would have done, as he afterwards told me, had not McGuffie seemed to read our very thoughts on the instant and threatened suddenly towards us with the knife.

And suddenly again the knock was repeated—more loudly this time, and seeming more peremptory. And my heart leapt up when it was accompanied by a shout from outside:

"Open! Open there, I say! In the name of the King!"

The effect on the spies was galvanic. Rush scrambled to his feet, knocking over the low chair in the movement. McGuffie gave a low muttered oath, and I heard him murmur:

"Well, well, it's that way! The King, is it! We never expectit such grand company the night!"

Kabal stood back a pace and drew one of the two long pistols I had seen at his belt. Only Blackadder retained any semblance of complete calm. He laid a hand on Kabal's arm to restrain him and advanced a few steps into the corridor towards the outer door— and he was moving with the loose, doddering shuffle which we had always known for the gait of Mr. Abershaw.

An instant later it was Mr. Abershaw's voice we heard, quavering and distressed as it might genuinely have been under such circumstances.

"Who is it? What do you want?"

And the voice from outside:

"I'm sorry, sir. I had no wish to frighten you. Lieutenant Butterfield of His Majesty's Navy. I have an injured man here and must have immediate attention for him. Will you let me in with him?"

A pause. Then Abershaw's voice again:

"I—I must beg you will excuse me, Lieutenant. I would like to help—very much indeed. But I—I have been unwell myself——"

"I ask your pardon, sir. I must insist. You need do nothing and you need fear nothing. I want no more than admittance and shelter for this fellow of mine."

With a single nimble step, Blackadder was back at the entrance to the room. We saw his face twisted in the gleam of rage we were coming to know so well. He beckoned Kabal and whispered to him and the other nodded and crossed to McGuffie.

"Stay silent," he said to him hurriedly—and they were the first words we had heard him openly speak. "Stay silent. But as they come through you are to assist me, do you comprehend—you are to assist me to attack. . . ."

McGuffie nodded—and was, I believe, about to embark on one of his endless speeches. But at that moment the voice outside spoke again:

"I must beg you to delay no longer, sir! I demand that you open. I am an officer of the King."

Blackadder, for his part, had seized from a corner of the mantel a small sandalwood box. He hurriedly opened it—and donned with an adept haste the wig of grey hair it contained. In an instant, before our eyes, he was transformed into Mr. Abershaw completely —the stoop, the genial, mildly smiling face—all were there. And leaving the door only a little ajar, he went quickly into the corridor again.

"I'm coming—I'm coming, Lieutenant," we heard him say. "I'm sorry—I have not been well—I have not been at all well. . . ."

There was a fumbling at the locks and chains—as we had heard them earlier ourselves, when we had been admitted by Mr. Abershaw. The door swung back and we heard the tramp of boots across the threshold.

"Good—good. Thank you, sir." Thus the official voice. "Most unfortunate—sorry to have troubled you. Yours was the end house, you see—the nearest as we came into the village. . . ."

"I trust your man is not badly hurt, Lieutenant. How did it happen?"

"On the beach a moment ago. A scuffle with some smuggling fellows. Come, steady, man—steady. . . ."

All this went forward at the outer door, with sounds of footsteps and a general scuffling activity as, presumably, Butterfield dragged his wounded man forward. In the room, at the mention of the smuggling fellows, McGuffie drew his breath sharply.

"Garamond!" he muttered. "Garamond and Sharp! Have they been taken?"

Kabal set his fingers to his lips, stepping over with one swift pace to a position behind the door as it would swing open at the entrance of the others.

The movement in the corridor came nearer. Butterfield, as we heard, was still explaining as he came:

"I'm in command of the men at the inn by the shore —you may have heard. Been down there impressing fellows for His Majesty's Navy—now that war's broke out again he'll need 'em—plenty of 'em. Daresay you've heard the war has broke, eh? Word just came through—'bout an hour ago. Thomson and I saw a light, d'y'see—saw it from the inn just a half-hour past. Reckoned it must be smugglers and went out to tackle 'em—had heard a rumour, y'know, that it was one of their confounded Moonshine nights or what d'y'call 'em. They was just offshore and making fast out to sea. So we fired, d'y'see—and they fired, d'y'see, and there was Thomson with a bullet in him, d'y'see. . . ."

All this time the pretended Abershaw was murmuring his sympathy and plainly helping the Lieutenant forward with the wounded man. They were close to the door of the room, and in an instant it swung open to admit them. The man Thomson was sagged over the Lieutenant's shoulder, and he—the Lieutenant, a little man, with a beetling red face—was struggling gamely forward with him.

"Confounded nuisance the whole thing. Can't go losing fellows like Thomson—good man, y'know. Thought he was done for, but he's all right, I think. Needs a bit of care, of course. . . ."

By this time he was well into the room. Blackadder, behind him, eased the still form of the wounded man from his shoulders and set him in a chair. Butterfield straightened himself—and found himself staring full into the muzzle of Kabal's pistol.

"What the devil!——"

"I beg your pardon, Lieutenant. You will be good enough, I hope, to raise your hands."

It was Blackadder who spoke, striding forward and slipping the grey wig from his head.

"Who the deuce are you?" spluttered Butterfield, his red face glowing and puffing and seeming it would burst in his rage.

"It matters not in the least—the story is infinitely too complex. Will you give me your sword, Lieutenant Butterfield?"

"Deuce take it I won't, sir! Confound it, I'll give my sword to no man but my King!"

"Then I must take it—and I must ask you to believe that if you try to prevent me my friend here would not hesitate to shoot you through the heart."

"Devil take you, sir, you won't have my sword! I don't know what I've fallen into, but it ain't anything savoury from the looks of any of you!"

For a moment they stood confronting, the little Lieutenant as angry a figure in his different way as Blackadder was. The latter half-raised his arm in a gesture to Kabal—but on the instant there was a diversion as unexpected to me as it was to all the others.

Harry, ever since McGuffie had loosened his bonds, had stayed silent. But all the while, as he explained to me afterwards, he had been working at the rope behind his back, and a few moments before—at the very point of Butterfield's entrance—he had succeeded in freeing himself entirely. Now, with all attention focused on the Lieutenant—with even McGuffie turned away from us towards him—he sprang forward, and with a wild gesture of the arm sent the lamp spinning from the table—and, with the same movement, made to overturn the other and smaller lamp likewise.

"Quick, Tom—after me!" he cried. "The door!"

I leapt to my feet. My bonds were still a hindrance, but in a furious spurt of energy I stumbled forward, thrusting with all my might against McGuffie as I did so.

The darkness was now complete—and in it all was confusion. I had a blind notion where the door was and struggled towards it. There was a stab of flame from Kabal's pistol and the whine of the ball above my head—the shattering of an ornament on the mantel. McGuffie swore uglily in the darkness beyond and there was a bellowing further from Rush.

Hampered as I was by my bonds I stumbled blindly against someone—and felt myself gripped closely. In a fury I fought to free myself, kicking and thrusting with my head—and heard close in my ear the pert furious tones of Butterfield:

"Deuce, it's you, boy! Who the devil's side are you on?"

"Outside—quick, outside!" I gasped. "Help me—help me!"

He grunted—but must have understood that we were

opposed to Blackadder as he was, and I felt myself pushing forward with him. In the darkness it was impossible to tell exactly where in the room we were but at the moment there was the sudden flare of a tinder match—and in its light we saw the frame of the doorway, the black corridor beyond—with, at the end of that, the outside door still unlocked as Blackadder had left it.

But it was Blackadder himself who had struck the match—and he stood before us, enframed in the doorway itself, filling it with his monstrous bulk.

"Confound you, sir!" bellowed Butterfield. "I don't know who the devil you are, sir, but you've caused me enough trouble to-night as it is, sir, and been the death of poor Thomson into the bargain more than like, sir! Get out of my way, sir!"

And as he bellowed the last at the top pitch of his voice, he thrust his bullet head forward and butted against the tall shape.

With a fierce, explosive gasp Blackadder fell back against the lintel. The match flew up from his hand and made an arc in the air across the room. In one last hasty glance back I saw in its light Kabal raise up his other pistol to aim at us, beyond him the white gaping faces of McGuffie and Rush. Then all was darkness again, and Butterfield and I were scrambling along the corridor. The outer door was open—left so by Harry as he had made his own escape, as we afterwards learned. We were through it instantly—and there, at the gate, was Harry himself, waiting for us.

From behind came angry confused shouts from the

cottage. We paused by the gate for only a moment while Butterfield, still grunting angrily, undid the last strands of my bonds.

"Deuce take it all, what's the meaning of it?" he was saying.

"They're spies, sir," said Harry breathlessly—"Spies! Blackadder—it's the famous Blackadder himself. We found out earlier and he took us prisoner. We must get down—we must get away—quickly—they'll be after us any moment."

And indeed on the instant there was a great cry from the cottage and we saw Blackadder himself at the outer door, outlined in the moonlight. He was pointing to us furiously as we stood at the gate. But as he and the others plunged forward towards us the bonds fell away from my hands. Harry had already taken to his heels—was a dark fleeting shape along the road that led to the shore; and in an instant Butterfield and I were after him, tearing at the last knot of my loosened gag as we ran.

"Make for the inn," gasped Butterfield. " The inn along the shore. I have men there. By St. Jupiter and all the saints I'll settle with these devils! Spies, eh! —spies! My name's George Butterfield, I was born in Kent, I'm a Lieutenant in His Majesty's Navy and my mother was an Englishwoman! Deuce take 'em all for a pack of scurvy knaves, but I'll settle with 'em yet! "

He delivered this incredible speech in a perfect bombastic fury, gasping it out word by word as we ran. In the complete unexpected humour of it in the circumstances in which we found ourselves—in the whole glory of the sudden freedom—in the excitement of the chase—I could not but laugh aloud to the sky as I raced forward through the night, the Lieutenant waddling with unexpected agility by my side, the scurrying dark shape of Harry before me, the streaming spies behind . . . .

A Shot in the Dark

We reached the beach, skirting down through the fields to the right, and sheltered as we went by a long low copse which spread over that part of the coast. Our aim, of course, was to make for the inn, the *Sheaf of Wheat*, where, as Butterfield had said, some men of his were billeted.

It was vital for Blackadder to attempt to recapture us, if all his secret was not to be disclosed. It had been his aim, as we learned afterwards from McGuffie, to continue as Abershaw for some time even after the actual outbreak of war, so that he could get vital information about our troop and fleet movements across the Channel. If he found us and either killed us or kept us out of the way, he could still do so; if we once got fully free, or could tell what we knew to others, he would have no alternative but to get out of the country as fast as he could.

He was like a madman as he pursued us, as McGuffie told us later. He realised that with Butterfield in our company we would indeed make for the inn. He ran after us in a silent ecstasy of ferocity, outstripping all his companions—certainly McGuffie and Rush, although the lithe Kabal was able to make some pace with him.

They lost sight of us in the copse—as it so happened took a false turn at one point here, and so lost the trail. We were able to make the beach unobserved; and, with the sounds of the chase now faded, we paused for a moment's breath and to reconnoitre our position.

We were breathless from our headlong flight—Butterfield indeed in a state of near collapse, his face positively a bright scarlet. But a moment or two in the shelter of some dunes set us straight, and we were ready again to go forward.

In this breathing space, of course, we explained to the Lieutenant exactly what had happened—our narrative constantly interrupted by his explosive interjections. He was in a fury against Blackadder for having trapped him at the cottage—in a greater fury against himself for allowing himself to be trapped; and, in the midst of all, evidenced the utmost human concern for his man Thomson, left wounded and unattended.

"Egad, I'll have the hide of that fellow Blackadder! —deuce take it if I don't! Posin' as a music-master, eh? Ha! Never did like music—can't bear long-haired fellows and such—might have known that chap was up to no good! "

Yet he seemed in no way interested in what to us was the real marvel of that evening's work: the coincidence, happy for us beyond all measure, of his choice of Abershaw's cottage to take shelter in.

"Had to find somewhere, confound it," he barked. "Couldn't leave the poor fellow lying—might as well, though, for all the good it's done him after all. . . ."

And so we edged forward, hugging the line of the dunes—sometimes cutting behind them to crouch our way through the marsh-land which lay at that point between us and the inn. That building was perhaps half a mile away from us—on this side of the harbour. It stood in a complete little isolation on a freak table of rock on the shore itself, and so had its own small natural jetty.

"Now see here," said Butterfield as we went, speaking always jerkily and on the breath: "The thing is, we want to tell the lads at the inn what's what—there's some half dozen of 'em there and a tough crew—need tough fellows for the impressing game—sometimes have to act rough if some fellow or other don't want to take the King's shilling. Now then: the chances are this man Blackadder has a sizeable ship not far away. That gig that Thomson and I fired at couldn't never have crossed the Channel by itself——"

(With this I instantly agreed—I had indeed myself formed the impression that there must be a larger craft than the gig not far from shore that night—the gig had only brought the two final boxes of pigeons in from it: plainly, with the war so close, Blackadder had decided not to run any real Moonshine that night and so had not called out the full gang—only his four immediate helpers, to assist him in getting in the consignment of birds.)

"Very well, then," went on the Lieutenant. "Point is there's a frigate of our own anchored not far away—the *Hawk*—'bout half-a-mile off-shore. Right. What we do is get to the inn, send one of my lads there to look after Thomson, send another of 'em up to Squire Westwood to get the militia out so as we can try to collar this Blackadder fella. Then I take the others out in the longboat we have at the inn. We find the *Hawk* —and we chase this other boat of Blackadder's with that. Reckon it can't have gone far yet—and I warrant it's full of messages from that devil that oughtn't never to get to France, I say!"

We nodded our complete agreement. For myself, I knew that my duty was to my mother—that as soon as we did reach the inn, and had put the matter completely in the hands of the authorities, my next step in all conscience was to go home. But I felt—as Harry did too, as I found—that we had begun this thing, and so would see it through. I decided that as far as I was concerned I would not rest until I had persuaded Butterfield to let us go with him in the longboat to the *Hawk*—and that I would stay with the *Hawk* in its turn until we had rounded up as many of Blackadder's spy ring in the other ship as we could.

And so we went on. Behind us, all signs of the chase had died; and as we came in active sight of the inn we broke cover and ran across the last quarter-mile of sand to the gaunt, huddled shape of the building. It was when we had almost reached it that a shot rang out, sheering brilliantly through the heavy stillness of the night. The ball whined between Harry and me, ploughing a path in the sand a few yards beyond us. We turned in our flight and saw Blackadder for a moment outlined against the wild sky on an uprising of ground near the marsh. He had plainly made separately for the inn in the hope of cutting us off. But he was too late. The shot was his last defiant gesture; and even as we sped forward again it was to see his twisted shape turn away and merge in the shadows. . . .

The Jetty

Ten minutes later it was arranged exactly as the Lieutenant had decided. He, in a frenzy of importance and fury, bustled about in the common room of the inn where his men were gathered—a grim, ferocious collection of ruffians, led by an old seaman who passed by the name of Blue Nose.

"You, Fraser—up to the last house on the right at the end of the village—kind of cottage place—dovecotes and things all round it. You'll find Thomson there. See him straight. Merton, up to Squire Westwood's as fast as ye can, man—tell him all I've told you and have him get his militia out. Scour the country—this fellow Blackadder—he's to get him—those other ruffians of his too. Quince——"

(At which Blue Nose himself stepped forward, touching his brow)—

"—Quince, into the longboat with the rest of the men. We're for the *Hawk*, my man—and deuce take it if there ain't a sea-chase before the night's done, and a rascally Frenchie for a prize. Step to it, men!"

And all was instantly a buzz of activity. Harry and I, regaled a little and recovered from our exertions and excitements by some ale from the astonished landlord of the *Sheaf of Wheat*, automatically went forward to join Butterfield and Blue Nose in the longboat; and the Lieutenant, in all his own excitement, seemed to take no exception to the move.

We felt suddenly immensely exhilarated—the night, which had begun so badly for us, was to end in triumph after all, it seemed. All our earlier resolutions came back—we felt ourselves bent upon important adventure—adventure which, moreover, was to be of some service to our country, now at war. We crowded behind the others as they made for the side door of the inn, leading out to the small jetty where the longboat was moored.

The one thing, the one thing only which marred our pleasure, was the thought that Blackadder himself would in all likelihood escape us. He had seen us enter the inn a good quarter of an hour before—he must know that there was now no other chance for him but immediate escape; and the probability was that at that very moment he was making away from the district with Kabal and the two others. The only hope left was that Squire Westwood might take him with the militia; but by the time our man reached Westwood, by the time Westwood assembled his men, a good half-hour at the least would have passed, and knowing our enemy it was unlikely that he would be within five miles of Lytchett by then.

As we advanced across the paving of the little quay

at the inn, the old seaman Blue Nose stopped for a moment and sniffed anxiously up at the sky.

"There's a deal of trouble coming up, sir," he growled. "Look at them clouds there, out seawards. And there's been thunder in the air this hour and more."

We followed his gaze, and saw indeed great scowling masses of black cloud piled up in vast turrets and battlements above the horizon. The air was sultry, as it had been all evening; and even as we stood there there came a far quiet rumble of thunder again.

"Tush, it won't break yet," said Butterfield impatiently. "Deuce take it, what's a little foul weather in any case? All the better, say I—'twill hinder those rascally Frenchies and give us a chance to make 'em. Come on, Quince—there's no time to lose."

We went forward again—ourselves, Butterfield, Blue Nose (that is, Quince), and three others. The longboat was rocking gently to and fro at the jetty steps, and one by one we descended to it. The seamen settled at the oars, and Butterfield, always muttering and spluttering to himself, took the tiller, Harry and I crowding close in the stern beside him.

We made ready to push off—Blue Nose was on the point of loosing the painter. And on the instant, in the heavy silence, I heard a low and evil sound which I had not thought to hear again that night—nor indeed wished ever to hear again, except in my most troubled dreams.

Above us, standing calmly on the topmost step of the jetty, a pistol in each hand so that he covered both

Butterfield and Blue Nose, was Blackadder. And behind him, on the edge of the jetty itself, regarding us as quietly and almost detachedly as he was, were the others—Kabal and McGuffie and the oafish Rush.

"Your eternal servant, Lieutenant Butterfield," came the thin edgy tones, "—your eternal servant, sir! You will not object, I hope, to giving us a passage. With your escape I have little alternative but to leave the country—and what more ironically satisfying in all the circumstances but that you, of all people—and our energetic young friends too, of course—should assist me to leave it!"

"Deuce take it!" mouthed the Lieutenant, his face scarlet again. "Deuce take it, sir!"

"Deuce take it indeed, Lieutenant," said the other smoothly. "But not, I hope, before you and your friends have taken us to the ship which is anchored and ready for us a little off-shore. Our own ship, I may add, and on her way to France. Will you be so good, Lieutenant Butterfield?—bearing always in mind, my friend, that I shall have you covered at the heart with these pistols from start to finish, and that if you make one move I do not wish you to make—if you steer in any other direction but the one in which I tell you to steer—you will be shot like a dog!"

And, still smiling, he advanced down the steps; and a moment later all four were in the longboat, Black-adder himself crouched before us where we sat in the stern, his pistols indeed trained on Butterfield's heart.

Hunger

Now I remember of all things in that nightmare voyage in the longboat out from the *Sheaf of Wheat*— I remember above all things else of horror that might be remembered, that I was suddenly desperately hungry! It was an age ago, a long age since I had had the bowl of pease-broth my mother made me every night for supper. I had had a long day's digging at the trenches on the common, I had had a long night's agony of suspense and terror; and I sat there in the stern, with the grumbling Butterfield and the silent Harry beside me—and with the menacing dark figure of Blackadder before me—and thought of naught else but that I was ravenous!

Then suddenly I recalled that long before, in the afternoon, I had slipped a morsel of bread and cheese in the pouch of my belt—as I had been on my way to the sea to bathe. I felt for it hopefully—and as I made the sudden move Blackadder stiffened, and for a moment the little black eye of one of his pistol muzzles edged towards me. But when he saw the crushed and sodden package I drew out he smiled—and for a moment in the nightmare it was the old smile of Abershaw.

"A little mulled ale, Tom—ah, what would you not give for a little of my old mulled ale, Tom! The creature comforts—even at a moment like this, the creature comforts!"

I made no answer—was engaged in dividing the bread and cheese for myself and Harry. It was a pitiful mess, pressed out of all recognition by my weight on it as I had lain on the beach. It tasted of salt from the

D.

damp that had seeped through to it, and was grained with sharp particles of sand. But we ate it avidly and were thankful for the chance that had preserved it.

And, as we did eat, the enigmatic man before us was feeling within the folds of his cloak with his left hand, setting one of his pistols on his knee to do so. And in a moment, without a word, but still smiling he held out to us a slice of the shortcake with which he had so often regaled us. I could suddenly have shouted in a crazy laughter out across the sea! I hesitated for only a moment—then leaned forward and took the strange offering—almost snatched it! And he bowed slightly as if at a social occasion ere he picked up the pistol from his lap again. . . .

The Longboat

We went on, we went on. Kabal, in the bows, had struck a flint and lit a dark lantern—I was aware of its occasional glow. The heavy air was full of the creak of the rowlocks, the slow oppressed grunt of Blue Nose and the others as they pulled. And from somewhere amidships, fantastic in the dark silence, came the voice of McGuffie singing softly and even with a vein of strange tenderness:

> *O can ye sew cushions,*
> *And can ye sew sheets,*
> *And can ye sing balaloo,*
> *When the bairnie greets? . . .*

And as we went, as we drove forward at Blackadder's muttered instructions, we made into the huge heaped battlements of the thunder clouds which all along that night had loomed and threatened. The sea, which had been calm enough as we moved out from the little inn jetty, now heaved in a huge turgid swell—there was a sense of nightmare as we crested the vast oily undulations of it, swooping slowly into the troughs, as slowly climbing up again as a new long slope of black water confronted us.

To crown all, it began to rain—great ponderous drops at the first, rare and menacing. As they burst on face or hands they seemed actually warm—the whole still air was warm—oppressively so, and thunderous. The moon was lost now, the massed clouds hiding it; from where we sat we could see no more than a white wicked patch for Blackadder's face—the occasional dim outline of his crouching frame as we rose on a swell and he was held for an instant against the sky.

Then suddenly there was a low muttering from beyond his dark shape, and a cessation momentarily in the steady sound of the pulling. And Blue Nose was speaking from the darkness:

"There's trouble ahead, Mr. Butterfield, sir," he said —the words he had used as we had moved down earlier to the jetty. "We're for it, sir—we should hove to—or go back, sir. There's trouble."

"Devil take it!" came Blackadder's angry hiss. "You do what I tell you, man!—and if you have something to say you address me and not Butterfield. Do your work—or there will be trouble ahead and to spare! "

"The fellow's right," exploded Butterfield beside me. "Deuce, Blackadder—or whatever your scoundrelly name is—Quince knows what he's talking about! If he says trouble it's trouble, and confound it if I don't agree with him myself. I don't like this sea and this rain—they're too *slow* to my mind."

"If anything is too slow it's this longboat," said Blackadder, his voice an edgy menace in the dark. "Devil take you, Quince—pull—pull, do you hear! Kabal—Rush—see to them forward there. McGuffie, in the name of all I hold sacred, if you do not stop that singing I'll shoot you! "

There was a sudden cessation of McGuffie's low perpetual crooning—and a further low grumbling from amidships as Blue Nose and the others started to pull again. Beside me, Butterfield still muttered irritably:

"Where in the name of Jupiter is the *Hawk*? By George if the *Hawk* was only near!——"

But he knew as well as we did that the *Hawk* was in a different direction altogether—at the moment of leaving the jetty, and at Blackadder's command, we had headed directly away from the *Hawk* and towards the French ship anchored somewhere in the darkness beyond us. From what Blackadder, at the start of that nightmare voyage had told us, the ship—a three-masted lugger named the *Manon*—was instructed to wait at an agreed point well off-shore until two o'clock, only to leave in the chance of an emergency. It was evident that there had been some intention of further business that night—and indeed, as we learned afterwards, the aim was for Kabal to have crossed with her to France with some vital instructions from Blackadder to his fellow-spies on the other side—that is, if all had gone according to the original plan, with Blackadder still ensconced in Lytchett as Abershaw. . . .

We were by this time some half-hour on the sea, from the moment of our leaving the jetty; and Kabal returned to his point of vantage in the bows, was scanning the troubled darkness ahead for a sign of the lugger. And suddenly he gave a cry, weird and echoing across the silent sea, and stood up, the lantern aloft.

"*Manon!*" he cried. "*Manon! Là voilà!*"

Blackadder, in a sudden reaction, turned—it was as if the sudden white patch of his face before us had been overswept by a black cloak. I was aware, beyond the dim heaving bulk of our boat, of a faint glimmer of yellow light low down on the sea ahead, intermittently blanking and glowing as both the vessels rose and fell. But I saw it for no more than a fleeting instant for there was a sudden shout and commotion beside me as Butterfield plunged himself forward to grapple with the enemy at the moment of the distraction of his attention.

"The tiller, boy!" he shouted as he sprang. "Take the tiller! Ah, confound you, sir!—I'll have your rascally throat before I'm a minute older!"

It was impossible to see clearly what was happening. There was a cry from Blackadder and a sudden stab of flame as he fired one of the pistols. But Butterfield was atop him, and the shot went wild into the black night. For me, I stayed for a moment stunned in the suddenness of the development, then leaped and groped for the tiller which Butterfield had relinquished. I had it in a moment—felt the swinging resistance of it as the boat veered round in the swell. From forward there was a double commotion as Blue Nose and the others, hearing Butterfield's shout, stopped pulling and made to attack McGuffie and Rush. In the well of the boat before me—at my very feet—Butterfield and Blackadder were grappling grimly—at one point there was a stab of pain in my leg as the boot of one or the other drove hard against my shin. And then, with a suddenness that was appalling in the extreme, there was a chill and icy blast of wind across the boat, a monstrous crack of thunder, a fierce wild hissing driving in on us, and the storm broke. . . .

Tempest

Of the immediately following events I have the dimmest recollection. Since then, in the course of my long life, I have seen many storms, but there is none that I can recollect that had the dreadful, instantaneous impact of that my first one.

It was a freak—a nightmare. We had expected trouble, but no trouble coming so incredibly suddenly. One moment we rode the slow menacing swell, as I have described it, the rain falling in great heavy drops; the next, there was a lash as of whips, a kind of *bursting* of all the sky and all the sea surrounding us, and our breath went out from us as if at a cruel and unexpected blow.

The arm of the tiller was ripped from my hand—swung back on the instant and cracked against my ribs. The shoot of pain was intense—I cried out—screamed, I suppose; but felt the very sound snatched away from my lips in the blast of the wind that drove over us.

Before me, in the heaving darkness, there was confusion. The fighting had stopped in the tremendous and unexpected impact of the storm, each man grasping at the gunwales, the seats—anything that offered—in the instantaneous instinct of self-preservation. Butterfield, below me, groped at my leg—I was aware of him heaving himself up to my side, gasping and breathless. Under the blow from the tiller-arm I had slid across the stern-seat and huddled full upon Harry—and was aware as I fell of the tiller-arm still thrashing to and fro as the boat slewed helplessly round in the sudden vortex involving us.

I tried to shout to Butterfield—tried desperately to warn him, even in the terror of the moment. But words were impossible. In a sudden detachment of anxiety—strange and remote in that moment of utter confusion—I saw his dim shape as he raised himself towards the seat beside me. His head upraised for an instant above the level of the gunwale—I saw it sharply outlined against the sudden black shine of the sea; and the tiller-arm, swinging sharply round, caught him a full hard blow on the temple.

He opened his mouth—I saw his lips all writhing in

an agony close to my face; and I suppose he cried out, as I had done earlier; but it was no more than a silent pantomime against the roar and blast of the wind and rain as he heeled over towards us, dragging both Harry and me into the dark well below, where Blackadder himself still huddled.

It takes long to tell, but it lasted all but an instant. I was stunned and half-blinded by a searing knife-edge of salt water which had flung across the gunwale in my eyes. My ears were full of the scream of the wind. Beneath us, the longboat shuddered like a living thing in a torment as she drove helplessly forward. How it was that she did not capsize is now a marvel to me— I can only suppose that although the wind and the rain were intense in their ferocity, the sea itself was still in a comparative calm—beaten down, as it were, by the very fury of the elements. It could not last so—after the first horrific impact of the blast, as the storm worked itself to its uttermost frenzy, the sea would burst and lash itself in huge jagged waves that would overwhelm us and smash us to a matchwood. But before then—before the great ravenous beast that surrounded us (the black water its body, the wind its icy breath)—before it could rise so in its wrath, there came salvation—if indeed it might be called salvation. . . .

We had all the time been driving helplessly forward, as I have said—and at a speed which I can in no way convey in poor words. As I recovered to a degree from the first stunned impact, I struggled to raise myself from the well of the longboat, where I lay heaped with

Harry and Blackadder and the unconscious Butterfield. My arm seemed wrenching out of its socket as I gripped at the gunwale to pull myself up. I was still dazed, but the blindness had left me. In my half-unconsciousness I still recollected to keep my head away from the tiller-arm, lest it still thrashed.

I dragged to my knees—and, on the instant, all was illumined by a great flash of lightning. It lasted the briefest fraction of a second, but in a sudden return of the strange far mood of detachment, I saw with an instantaneous clarity the whole wild scene. It burns still in my brain as I write, as if engraved forever from that terrible moment on the tablets of my memory.

We were deep in a trough of black shining water—the sides of it heaved up from us like the tortured flanks of a great animal. Our prow was already mounting to the rim of this mighty saucer. In it, erect, was the tall thin figure of Kabal, one hand held high and pointing, his hair streaming out like a black flag. Amidships was a confusion of bodies in a tormented huddle—I was aware, from out the dark shapeless mass of them, only of the round blank gaping face of McGuffie, the mouth sagged open, the eyes in a daze of incomprehension. One oar jutted up from the midst of the mass like a mast, the blade of it shattered across in a splintered diagonal. . . .

All this I saw in that one instant of light—and more. Beyond Kabal, high up on the rim of the black saucer in which we wallowed, its masts dipped crazily in an angle towards us, its black hulk glistening, was the French lugger *Manon*. And we drove towards it implacably, speeding forward as if winged before the driving fury of the wind.

Death

And now indeed, looking back across the years, it seems to me that a miracle did befall that night at the point of impact between the two vessels—our longboat from the *Hawk* and the French lugger *Manon*. At the least, in that sea, in that hurricane of wind, we might have expected, every one of us, to have been maimed in some way for life, if not killed outright; as it was, we lost but two men—Blackadder's lieutenant Rush, and one of Blue Nose's companions, a man named Corinth, who died later on board the *Manon* herself.

So dazed and confused were we by what we had gone through since the outburst of the storm, that we hardly realised for some time that the collision had taken place. I had seen the two vessels rushing together in the sudden bright flash of the lightning—but it had seemed to me that a great space still separated us. Yet it was a bare instant after the flash of lightning that I grew aware of a sudden fierce shudder all through the longboat—with, simultaneously, borne back to me on the rushing wind, a great long-drawn scream from the prow—from Kabal. It was indeed, that scream, the first human sound that I had heard since the storm began—all else had been a turmoil of sea and wind and rain.

And then, for a long moment, there was an uncanny stillness. The wind howled, it is true, and the rain lashed down still; but there was a weird cessation of all *movement*—the longboat held quite rigid, all the vibration which had run through her as we speeded across the sea gone out like the breath of life itself.

Then and only then—a whole eternity after what must have been the moment of impact itself—did I hear a harsh and rending splintering; and the boat gave a wild last lurch which threw me forward from my knees.

What had happened, as we afterwards reckoned it, was that by some uncanny chance, as our boat drove into the lugger, her bows had reared themselves high above the sea-line. The *Manon*, in common with most French luggers of the time, was a squat and low-built vessel, lumpish in her line. All round her hull there was a projection—an out-thrust from her spar-deck—a kind of *bumper*. And our little boat, thrust forward by the immense pressure of the wave on which we rose, the force of the wind behind us, had splintered herself forrard against this projection. In the fury of movement her bow-strakes had opened and gauped like a mouth—had held thus for a moment; and, as the lugger heeled, and the sea fell away from under our own keel, had jammed so and interlocked, so that we jutted out from the side of the *Manon* like an outrigger.

All this held for only an instant; then, as the lugger heeled over, we struck the surface of the sea with a great explosive crack, and a deluge of icy water swept over us.

Yet even then, in that blind moment, we all felt,

instinctively, that in some way we were attached to the *Manon*—how, we could not yet grasp, for we did not work out the detailed shape of the movement itself, as described above, until afterwards; but somehow we did feel it—and were already, all of us, scrambling forrard to reach the larger vessel. Meantime too, Kabal, in the bows, had managed to shout to some of the crew of the *Manon*, clinging to the bulwarks, that Blackadder was on board us. His (Kabal's) right arm had been shattered at the moment of impact—it was why he had screamed; but his courage and tenacity were superb—I admit it even of an enemy. With an admirable presence of mind, one of the Frenchmen on the lugger threw a grappling iron down towards us— yet it was that very gesture which destroyed Rush. He was near the bows, near Kabal; and, as the grappling iron fell, it caught him square across the chest (this we learned later from Kabal who was near him, while we still struggled forrard from the stern). Rush, in what must have been an agony as the spikes of the iron bit into his flesh, swept over the gunwale of the long-boat; but even in that dreadful moment the blind devotion which Blackadder somehow could inspire in his men made him cling with a fearful strength to the gaping forward strakes. Those massive, animal arms of his wrapped round and clenched us; and he was, for one prodigious instant, at the moment when the long-boat was easing itself away from the lugger with the second fall of the sea, a veritable living anchor—a man already doomed, but straining every last brute nerve to save the master he somehow loved.

As for ourselves in that brief passage in the longboat, Harry and I, by an instinctive collective action, were struggling desperately with the almost helpless form of Butterfield. He had to an extent recovered consciousness but not fully—and was almost a dead weight upon us as we lumped forward in the darkness. Blackadder had already gone forward, had met with McGuffie— we heard, even above the chaos of wind and sea, the Scotsman's great bellowing:

"Maister—Maister! Haud here, man—oh, haud here!" And Kabal, too, despite his useless arm, was supporting the great bulk of his leader. None of the spies cared what might happen to us—why should they?—yet it was one of our men who was the salvation of all of us. Old Blue Nose, a more experienced seaman than any other man aboard the longboat, had realised in an instant what had happened. With the man Corinth, who later died, he leapt upwards to the bulwarks of the lugger—where already some storm-lanterns were dimly glimmering as the panicky crew assembled, clinging to stanchions, shrouds, backstays —anything they could lay hands on. In the wild darkness, Blue Nose and Corinth set blindly to help aboard any who presented themselves, friend or foe. And the first so helped were Kabal and McGuffie with the near-unconscious Blackadder. Then came one of the other seamen from the *Hawk*, the third—the last of our own small crew—having made his own way across the lugger's bulwarks; and finally ourselves—Harry and I with the helpless Butterfield. Soaked, blinded, gasping —almost lost—we found ourselves at the last caught up in the strong arms of Blue Nose and Corinth and dragged up and over, only to fall floundering thereafter on the lugger's heaving deck.

It was in this last moment of all that Corinth received the wound which destroyed him. In leaning forward to seize us he slipped and half-toppled over the gunwale again; and at this instant (as he told us later before his death) he saw, in the pale downward glow of one of the lanterns, that Rush had reached the end of his tether. The brute (he was no more—*could* have been no more, to do what he did do) was virtually already dead. The grappling iron was deep embedded in his chest. His small pig-eyes were glazed—upturned in his skull. In some dim way, perhaps, he realised that all was over— that his beloved master was aboard and safe; and so he relinquished at last his Herculean grasp on our forward strakes. On the instant the wild sea broke—a monstrous wave swept upwards, caught the shattered longboat and tossed it like a toy. It remained high-poised for the briefest instant, and slewed round, catching Corinth a great blow across the head; then slid with a last broken shudder, like a stricken animal, into the blackness beyond. The agonised Corinth staggered back and fell in a slithering heap across the deck of the lugger; and so saw no more of what might have happened to Rush. But, much later, when all was over, and the *Manon* was a bleak forlorn wreck herself (as will be described in due course of time), we saw the grappling iron dangling still from its bulwarks; and wrapped tight round one of its cruel spikes, a little bloodied rag—a fragment from Rush's shirt.

Thus perished, then, the first of Blackadder's immediate companions. Would that his devotion had been inspired by a better master!

In the Hold

And so went on the long nightmare of that night. A century before Harry Rowan and I had gone swimming in the little cove near peaceful Lytchett—a lifetime past we had sauntered with Philadelphia, Harry telling us disjointedly that ancient story of his early days, of his escape from France at the time of the Revolution. We had seen our whole world topple, he and I, in the moment of our recognition on the beach of Abershaw as Blackadder; and we had lived through an eternity of suspense and danger in the flight to the inn with Butterfield and the nerve-racking voyage in the lost longboat.

And now we lay in the hold of the *Manon* while the storm still raged above us. It was a dim and fearful scene, and I remember it in uttermost clarity till this day.

In the faint swinging glim of a lantern we crouched all together there, friends and foes side by side, but all dominated by the great still figure of Blackadder. He sat on an upturned brandy-pin at the foot of the little companionway—and somehow, despite the violent and continuous lurching of the lugger, he maintained a kind of immobility and dignity. In the mêlée in the longboat his pistols had gone; but he had a musket from one of the crew of the *Manon*, and sat with it across his knee. His face was alabaster in its whiteness, strained and drawn from the bitterness of our experience on the open sea; but he occasionally still smiled —that ancient twisted smile, the caricature of Abershaw's smile; and even against the howl and whine of the elements, he mouthed at moments the melody of the little Haydn Serenade.

By his side, sprawled out, his round face puffed and in a misery, was McGuffie. In the peril of the storm he had lost, it seemed, his eternal volubility; but occasionally, as the little ship lurched even more violently in the heaving sea, he would mutter and groan and seem even to be praying, if such a thing might be possible.

"Hech, mither, mither!" he grunted once. "Ye never kent, poor soul, the way your wayward lad would gang! I mind the days I played aboot the Lanark doors, and was a wee thing, innocent at your knee!—and I'm just an auld lost sinner now and the fear o' death in me, wumman, and wi' a hert a' wicked black wi' sin and tapsalteerie ways. What mercy can I expect— what mercy? . . ."

Kabal was deadly white. He lay back on a heap of sacking, his eyes closed, his face contorted in the pain from his shattered arm. McGuffie had bound it in a rude splint and sling. A beading of sweat was on the Frenchman's brow, his lips were tight-drawn.

Our own party huddled together opposite. Harry and I sat wedged in a corner to combat the movement of the ship. Butterfield's head was on my knees. He had fully recovered consciousness, but was strained and silent from the dreadful blow he had received from the swinging tiller-arm. The side of his face was one huge bruise, the skin broken just above the eye.

A little way across from us sat Blue Nose, his weather-tanned face quite expressionless. He accepted all with a bland and indifferent philosophy—good fortune and bad; it was his simple belief, as an old seaman who had seen much, had suffered much, that Providence knew best what was the most fitting destiny for Elijah Quince; and so he left it, never grumbling, never rejoicing.

The other three members of the longboat crew crouched beside him. Corinth lay on the floor, rolling helplessly back and forth in the movement of the ship despite the efforts of his two companions to steady him. He was unconscious—had fallen so not long after our arrival on board the lugger. His head was one vast open wound—the skull gaped wide above the ear. That he was not dead already was miraculous. One of his companions, a man named Joseph Wasp, a thin, tremulous little fellow, always, as it seemed, on the point of open tears (yet wiry and strong withal, as we often discovered), had contrived a rough dressing for the wound. He moaned to and fro over Corinth's still form, shaking his head and muttering:

"Ah, Johnny Corinth, Johnny Corinth! You was the handsomest sailor I ever did see, Johnny Corinth!—you was the best topsail man of the fleet, Johnny Corinth! And it was many the happy times we had, Johnny Corinth—at Pompey and such, and Barbados and Valparaiso. And now 'twill be a set sea-burial for you, old Johnny Corinth, and your messmate all alone for evermore! "

This quaint and whining dirge went on and on, mingling with McGuffie's occasional plaint and Blackadder's soft murmuring of the Haydn air; and all against a continuous background of the howling storm without, and the cracking thunder. How the crew of the lugger fared we did not know—in some ways we were almost past caring. At the start, the master had come down to us, to take orders from Blackadder—to pay his respects at least, for orders were of little value in that sea. He was a little, voluble, scared fellow of a Frenchman, oppressed with an immense sense of responsibility—baldheaded, ornate in his dress even at such a moment. He wore, fantastically, a kind of high fashionable stock above his white storm-jacket, and sodden though it was it had the effect of propping his head up, as if long before it had fallen from his body under a sheer weight of pomposity, and had been balanced on again, the stock serving to bind it unnaturally in place.

He gabbled interminably in French, nodding and bobbing, his eyes round-scared. And Harry (who naturally knew the outlandish tongue) told me after he had gone that he was explaining that somehow, above, they had contrived to storm-rig the lugger. Lying at anchor as she had been, she was fairly staunchly reefed at the outset; and fortunately one of the crew, who was more of a sailor than any of the rest, had seen the storm coming and they had partially prepared for it. They had contrived the rest somehow in the early stages—even while we were struggling aboard; although the taffrail had gone, and the flying-martingale, as the aft-mast had splintered at the first fierce blast of the wind. Now, there was no hope of being able to control the lugger's movements. The old seaman was at the wheel, struggling his best to steer us towards the Normandy Coast. But there was little chance of success—we were sweeping out of control in the blast of the wind and sea in a direction of S.S.W., towards, in short, the open sea. . . .

And so the hours went by. At intervals, a cascade of green icy water would gush down the companionway —as we lay there we were periodically drenched all over again, no matter how we turned. Towards dawn, the storm seemed to ease slightly—but still howled, and still was merciless. A filter of pale light seeped in at a porthole above our heads, mingling strangely with the fitful glim of the swinging lantern. And at the moment there was a strange high womanish cry from Wasp:

"Dear heart! Ah, dear heart! Oh, Johnny Corinth, Johnny Corinth! "

The loglike form of Corinth suddenly convulsed— half-raised itself. The dressing fell away from the huge raw wound in the head. For an instant he stayed so, on his face an expression all baffled and forlorn and then he fell back. Wasp shuddered and hid his little weary eyes. And there was a moment of comparative silence—filled only with Blackadder's implacable humming of the Haydn melody. He made no sign of compassion—even of recognition of the presence of death. His countenance was remote and expressionless —except for its constant twisted gleam of evil.

But McGuffie shadowed over with a sudden little contortion of something like fear; and whispered softly:

"Oh, Lord, hae mercy! Good Lord!—hae mercy! . . ."

Conclusion

And so my present part of the chronicle draws in towards its end. I have undertaken, in this my own writing, to deal with the events of that first long night; thereafter it is Harry's task to continue the adventure. But before I do set aside my pen, for the moment at least, I must try to reconstruct a fragment of conversation which has some bearing on much that befell hereafter.

It was still in the grey light of dawn, with the storm dying somewhat—an hour, perhaps, after the death of John Corinth. The little master of the lugger had come down to us again, more scared than ever; and had told Blackadder that he had no idea where we might be—heading towards land of some kind, he hoped, but all true bearings were impossible. The dozen men of his crew were exhausted—utterly exhausted; the experience was unlike anything they had encountered before. With the exception of the old man at the helm, they none of them were real sailors—their main experience in the past had been of little more than runs to and fro across the Channel on calm Moonshine nights.

When he went, shaking his pompous little head, so that it seemed it might fall from the stock indeed,

Blackadder stayed silent for a long time, brooding. Then, unexpectedly, he looked across to where Harry and I were crouching together against the wall of the hold. Butterfield had fallen into an uneasy sleep across my knees—and soaked and cramped though I was, I was contriving to disturb him as little as possible.

"De Rohan," said Blackadder abruptly. "Come here, boy—here to me."

Harry looked at him dully, hardly comprehending. He was weak and stunned—as I was, indeed, from all we had been through. He half-shook his head.

"Come here, I say!" snarled Blackadder; and made a sudden half-gesture with the gun on his knee.

Harry crawled forward, not trusting himself to stand upright in the constant heaving of the ship. He crouched thus at Blackadder's feet, the enigmatic figure of our enemy looking down at him in the sick, yellow-green light.

"You embarked on more than you knew, boy—you and Cathro—when you came to spy on me. The marvel is you still live—either of you. You might have died in all we have gone through—you might have died before we ever came as far as this—on the beach, when I found you. . . ."

He stopped; and suddenly reached down his hand and seized Harry at the neck, twisting his head up towards him. His face was intent and ferocious.

"Do you know why you did not die, de Rohan?— that time on the beach? Do you know what it was that Kabal there whispered to me at the moment when I could have shot you?—yes, and Cathro too, because you had dared to follow me and spy on me?"

Still Harry said nothing. He has told me since that he was held by those deep-hard eyes of our enemy like a man mesmerised. They seemed to search full into him, and bar him from all movement.

"Because," went on the enemy in a low hiss, through his teeth, "—becase *you are who you are*! Because Kabal reminded me at the moment that you *were* de Rohan, and the last of your line! Because, my friend, when I came into your part of England, I was not thinking only of serving my country—but of serving myself! Because I had an old score to settle—which I would have settled in due time if all had gone as I had planned it should have gone. . . . Why do you think that Abershaw wearied himself with the company of two boys —when there were a hundred other things for Abershaw to think of? Why did I pander to you, boy, and have you to my house through all those months when it was a danger for me to have anyone in my house? Because you were who you are—again because of that! Because ten years ago—more than ten—you made a deadly enemy and did not know it!"

All this he said in an intense low whisper, which still cut through the sound of the storm and reached my ears across the hold. He spoke not continuously, in one speech as I have written it down here, but in swift broken sentences. Now he made a pause longer than usual, and twisted Harry's head closer towards him.

"I would to heaven," he said, his voice rising, "—I would to heaven it was never you I had with me on this devil's trip! I would to heaven it was your grandfather I was taking to France! But I swear that when this is over, and when I have done all else I have to do, I shall still reach your grandfather—through you! Ten years ago he escaped from me—you all escaped from me, when I had worked with every fibre of me to bring you and your line to justice. Two died indeed —but two still live. And more than that, one or other of you knows something I would give my very soul to know! "

Against a sudden increase in the power of the storm he was almost screaming. McGuffie was gaping up at him in a kind of foolish astonishment. Even Kabal had opened his eyes and slewed round his head to regard his master.

"Somewhere—somewhere there is an answer to the secret I have sought for ten long years!—and which I would have wrung from that old man when all was ready—when my other tasks were done and Abershaw set aside. You know, boy—one or other of you knows——"

But on the instant, as we stayed there in a fascination regarding his twisted, insane face, there was a great and violent shudder through all the ship—a huge crashing and splintering of wood; and, from the decks above, a wild screaming and shouting. The hatch of the hold burst open and a cascade of white seething water drenched in on us. We were thrown and huddled against the walls—I felt my shoulder shoot through with pain as I was thrust sideways on a bulkhead.

Then all went blank for me—a great cold blackness

closed in on my mind. I recall no more than a kind of hapless bewilderment which went all through me as I saw, in the pale light, the corpse of John Corinth swing upwards in the impact and remain propped for a moment against the wall. And then the darkness closed indeed and for a long long while I knew no more. . . .

PART THREE

"CRIBBED, CABIN'D AND CONFINED"

The story continued from the point of the wreck of the MANON

by

Mr. Henry Rowan

Head of the House of Rowan and Sons, Wine Merchants, of London, and rightful Chevalier de Rohan-Soubise.

CHAPTER THE FIRST

I: INTRODUCTORY

IT FALLS to me now, as per agreement with my friend, Sir Thos. Cathro, to proceed with the account of our adventures in the years gone by.

I do so with diffidence. I am no writer, but a plain man of business. He, I believe, *is* something of a writer; takes some pride at least in practising the art; as all the world knows has distinguished himself with some notable contributions to Letters, namely his *Narrative of a Voyage to the Great Loo-Choo Island* and his *Fragments of Voyages and Travels in the Years* 1820, 21 and 22, *Chiefly for the Use of Young Persons.*

He has also written an account of that part of our own adventures as boys which fell on the first day and night of the Second War with Bonaparte—i.e., the day and night of May 18th, 1803.

You may judge from that whether he is able to write or not. I hold that it is a graphic and moving description (I may, however, be biased).

For my part I am a plain man of business. It is a paradox that I, who have French blood, should be the practical and reserved one; while he (Sir Thos. Cathro), priding himself upon being a bluff man-o'-war's man, and very blunt and hard-headed, should be the more romantic.

This, however, is the case; and the way of life.

Moreover, the part of the adventure which he has described concerned one brief period of time, and there was much colour in it. For my part, I have to write upon a period of long and slow movement.

Therefore, there will be a marked difference in manner in the two episodes. I relate facts, no more; avoiding too elaborate a use of colour; for I am a plain business man, as I have said.

With these Introductory Remarks I now proceed:

II: WE ARE CAST UP UPON THE SHORE OF BRITTANY

It will be recollected how we were held captive of Simon Blackadder of ill memory upon the French barque *Manon*. We were driven by a raging storm out of course. On the morning of May 19 we were forced upon rocks near the fishing village of St. Pol-de-Leon.

A great commotion broke out when we struck. We in the hold were cast *nolens-volens* in all directions; some of us being badly bruised. My friend, Tom Cathro, was made insensible by a blow in the shoulder and head from a bulkhead.

For my part, I was hurled against Simon Blackadder, he toppling from the brandy-pin upon which he had been resting. The others were likewise cast hither and yon.

From the deck above there was much shouting. The Master of the vessel appeared at the burst hatch and cried down to us (in French) that we were struck, there was no hope, we must toil every man for himself, etc.

We made what exeunt from the hold we could, I assisting my friend Tom. Lieutenant Butterfield helped me too, having by this time recovered full consciousness, but in pain from the blow at his head.

We had, we discovered on deck, beat over a great reef of rocks. Our rudder was unshipped and there was much damage to the ship's bottom. She therefore made a great deal of water. There was no hope for her succour.

The gale still blew, but the storm to an appreciable extent had lessened. In the drive of rain and mist, we perceived that landing would be possible. Some of the *Manon* people were foolishly and hopelessly at the pumps. Three of the crew had been swept overboard and drowned at the moment of the wreck.

With great difficulty we made our way ashore and over the slippery rocks. The last of us was barely off when the ship reared high and slithered from her resting place; and so tossed haplessly in the seething cauldron of the sea, and cracked afresh upon another barrier of the reef further out. One foolish man still laboured at the pumps; and looked very surpris'd and threw up his arms; and then went out of view and so died.

The rest of us staggered up the beach beyond the rocks. There we found some fisher cottages. Simon Blackadder leading us, we entered and roused the people to make us refreshment. This they did in trembling before the wicked figure of the Spy: he was ever at his best, or worst? when threatening.

Tom was restored to consciousness by some brandy. And so we remained in those cottages until the morning was advanced and the storm had died. We were a large party, and in the predominance of Blackadder's people there was no hope of our own men being able to do aught. Of us there were the following: Myself; Tom Cathro; Lieutenant Butterfield; the seaman Quince (known as Blue Nose); the seaman Wasp; and another seaman, Driffield. Of Blackadder's crew there were: Blackadder; Louis Kabal; the Scotsman, Habbakuk McGuffie; the Master of the *Manon*, one du Parc; and some eight men of the *Manon's* crew, a ruffianly and derelict set, all very wet and frightened.

III: AN UNCOMFORTABLE JOURNEY

In the afternoon, with a fisherman for guide, we made on foot for St. Pol-de-Leon. We were a straggled and distressful spectacle as we went forward, Blackadder leading, Kabal and McGuffie at the rear, armed, to prevent us in any escape.

I recall that this man McGuffie (a strange fellow, with whom we grew friendly as the time went on) had recaptured his high spirits. He joked and laughed as we walked, reciting much poetry and indulging in reminiscence upon a Scottish poet he had known in his earlier times, one Robert Burns.

"Ah, Rabbie, Rabbie," he sighed at one point, "if you could but see me now! We twa hae played aboot the braes and pu'd the gowans fine. . . . Man, look at me! Stotting about here in a foreign land and fair ashamed o' mysel'. It's a terrible ploy this I'm on. I doubt ye wouldnae want to speak to me, Rabbie—and you and me so sib once! Hech, hech! "

But then he recovered his spirits in a moment thereafter, and embarked upon a long poem of one Shanter, who had been involved in a pursuit of witches. An uncouth poem it seemed to me at the time, and singularly inappropriate for recitation at our present pass.

At St. Pol we were thrown into jail—I mean, our own set. Blackadder forthwith presented himself to the Maire and disclosed his name and business. It was his aim, it seemed, to get to Paris, to report there to his superiors (if indeed the man had superiors—it was he himself was the superior; to report then to his colleagues, I should say). And so plans were laid for a journey which I remember in some distress.

It so happened that a body of conscripts, recruits and volunteers was about to set out to Paris from St. Pol, war now having broken. And it was agreed that we should travel with this horde.

Two days later, early morning, we assembled in the square outside the jail. We were restored to some health by our rest, and by the food, meagre though it was, which we had received.

The recruits numbered some score and a half of rough fisher-fellows, some armed, others with a foolish collection of swords and various knives—one with a scythe. Blackadder had been provided with a horse—a black gaunt animal, as sinister as himself. Kabal, his wounded arm in a sling, rode also—a sorry aged mare. McGuffie and du Parc were ensconced in a rough wooden chariot or cart—a kind of tumbril; with some supplies and such. There were several of these carts, carrying women and children—the wives and in some cases the sweethearts of the recruits, who insisted upon travelling with them to Paris.

The recruits and ourselves were to walk. And so we set off, the village turning out in force to cheer us—or rather to cheer their own people; we for our part were booed, and even openly stoned, as hated Englishmen. It was as one of the stones sailed narrowly near his already wounded head that the good Butterfield turned upon the crowd.

"By George," he bellowed, his face all puffed up as it was wont to do, "—by *George*, which is the name of myself and the name of my King and the name of the patron saint of the country I serve—by *George*, you may have the whip hand now, but the day will come when we infest your wretched den here and drub you till you wish to heaven you had never paid heed to the wicked wretch of a Bonaparte who leads you! Deuce take it if we don't—and God bless Admiral Nelson!"

At which we others raised a cheer. And so we went forth, not ungallantly, I think; and our wretched journey began.

We camped at nights in fields and woods, or billeted ourselves forcibly upon farmers and smallholders or the authorities of the various towns we passed through. We made reasonable pace, considering all things. Within two days, however, both Tom and I were badly knocked up from sore feet—and Butterfield too, a man unaccustomed to arduous exercise on land, was much distressed.

All the time as we went, Blackadder rode at the head of our cavalcade, alone and enigmatic. He was a bleak and saturnine figure upon his huge black horse. He spoke to no one—only occasionally upbraiding the irrepressible McGuffie, who talked constantly. For my part, I was deeply intrigued and not a little frightened by the speech he had made to me in the hold of the *Manon*. What had he meant?—that I had "made an enemy and did not know it?" Why would he have preferred my grandfather to be with him instead of me? Why indeed had he not killed us upon the beach? —because I *was what I was*, as he put it?

And then, at the thought of my grandfather, my emotions clouded over and in the extremity of physical suffering as we went forward I could have wept too from heartfelt sorrow. I thought of the poor old man back at Lytchett—I thought of his discovery, probably at the very moment of our landing at St. Pol, that I was not in the house. He would, I knew, be half-demented in my continued absence—he loved me not only (as I believe) for myself, but because of my position as last of the line of our branch of the de Rohans.

Tom too, I knew, was concerned for his mother. She also would be distressed beyond measure by the loss of her only son. We wished desperately that we might somehow convey to our people that we were alive at least, if not totally safe.

And all the time too, at the back of my mind, was a

E.

lingering impression—a faint memory; that I did half-know what Blackadder had meant. It was an elusive fancy from far-afar-off—a name, I think, or a phrase of some kind, that once I had heard. . . .

Blackadder himself made no sign of continuing the matter. Once or twice, when we had stopped for the night somewhere, perhaps, I found him looking at me very strangely. On one occasion he moved forward, scowling and black, as if to speak; but turned away with an angry exclamation to McGuffie, who at that moment had started to sing in his usual raucous way.

IV: A NEW FRIEND, AND AN ATTEMPT AT ESCAPE

As the weary days went by, they were enlivened to some extent by an acquaintance we made. This was a young girl of our own age who was travelling in one of the tumbrils. Her mother was with her. The girl's father was not with the recruits—he was already stationed as a soldier in a barrack at Paris. His two relatives were seizing the opportunity of the cavalcade to visit him there.

She was a charming girl, her name Mignonne de Barbaroux. She took pity on us as we went, passing down from the tumbril in which she travelled small dainties to relieve us. Once or twice, when it could be contrived, she helped us over the rail of the tumbril itself, and so we had a few stolen miles of comparative comfort.

We learned from her, surprisingly, that she had a

strain of English blood. Her grandmother had been a Cornishwoman, married into Breton fisherfolk stock, as often used to happen. Mignonne had a smattering of English—moreover, was in her heart (but secretly) no admirer of Bonaparte.

"He is but a tyrant," she whispered to us once. "I may not *say* so, but I think so, my friends. In his heart my father thinks so also—it is against his wish that he fights in the war with you—he is a soldier whether he like it or not like it. . . . Ah, it is hard for there to be such bloodshed always! We Breton people love peace, and Bonaparte will bring nothing but sorrow to our land. . . ."

It was Mignonne who helped us to attempt an escape. We were perhaps three leagues from Paris, encamped near the little town of Nonancourt. Blackadder had been met outside the town by a group of fellows dressed in a kind of uniform—not full-fledged soldiers, it seemed, but a kind of civil force of *gens-d'armes*, as they were called. He had ridden off rapidly with these, in close consultation with them. McGuffie informed us in his usual voluble way that this town was one of the headquarter places of Blackadder's spy ring—indeed, it was to here that some of the very pigeons from Mr. Abershaw's dovecotes had flown.

We settled for the night in a kind of circular camp, the tumbrils ranged all round, ourselves bivouac'd in the centre. We were much interested here by a spectacle which we could not but view with some thrill of excitement, even although it was a manœuvre of our country's enemy.

At some little distance away from us some French officers and soldiers were exercising with balloons.

We had heard rumours in England that Napoleon was much interested in the balloon as a form of military weapon. I have since those days looked into the history of it all (for a reason of interest which will be made clear in due time). It seems that as early as 1795 Bonaparte formed two companies of *aerostiers*. The notion was that two men went aloft in the basket of a huge tethered balloon filled with hydrogen gas, made on the field by passing sulphuric acid over iron filings. These two men were then able to survey from that great height all the preparations of the opposing army, and so bring back information and maps giving the secrets of all important troop dispositions, etc.

It was a group of these *aerostiers* that we now saw in training. The balloon itself, a vast sphere, floated high above our heads: we could make out the small toy-like figures of the aeronauts looking down upon us.

It was a notable sight. McGuffie, beside us, explained:

"Aye, aye, the Maister has aye been interested in such-like notions. He's a very curious man, laddies. He has a scheme for using they unholy things up there for mair than just observin', ye ken."

And he went on to tell us that Blackadder had always been a particular believer in the balloon; and that, together with his spying activities, he was evolving a plan for a great fleet of balloons to be used against England herself. The notion was that they would be loaded with bombs which would be controlled by time fuses; that they would be sent in a fleet across the Channel to London; that there the fuses would send the bombs raining down upon the Capital; that a further fleet of large balloons would be following on, full of trained troops; and that these troops would drop down upon the confused and terrified city by means of parachutes.

Fortunately, this terrible scheme was never developed in the Second Napoleonic War; but it is a real possibility that some day, in some war of the future, perhaps, fire and explosives will indeed rain from the sky, and trained soldiers descend in battalions from the clouds.

But to return:

McGuffie was in charge of us in that camp at Nonancourt in his master's absence. In his interest in the balloon, he moved some little distance away from us, leaving us quite alone by one of the empty tumbrils. It was at this moment that Mignonne suddenly appeared by my side.

"Quick," she said, speaking rapidly in French: "Now is the chance. Make for the woods and hide there. I shall set them on a false scent. . . ."

And she thrust two small packages into my hand. Why she should have helped our escape at that outset of our friendship I know not—only, I think, because she had pity upon us in our distress, was afraid of and hated Blackadder, and in her heart was secretly upon the English side.

I rapidly communicated to Tom and Butterfield what she had said. We looked round for the others, but Blue Nose, Wasp and Driffield were in another part of the camp, and so we could not wait for them.

With a last look to see we were unobserved, we darted beneath the carriage of the tumbril and ran rapidly for the woods. Butterfield and Tom were both badly lame from our long enforced walk, but despair lent us wings and we rushed for shelter.

In a small spinney we lay; and I opened the two packages: one contained food, the other (ah, feminine foresight!) long soft woollen stockings to guard our lacerated feet.

Instantly, from below us, we heard a commotion as our escape was discovered. We peered forth from cover; and saw Mignonne signalling to McGuffie that we had gone "such and such a way"—which was a direction totally different from our true one. The Scot and some of the recruits ran feverishly off—and we as quickly made across the little wood where we lay.

We burst forth from it on a stretch of deserted countryside, sloping down for perhaps a mile to a river. Tolerably certain that we would not be pursued, we descended; then skirted the bank for some distance; until we found a deserted mill-house. With a quick reconnaissance that it was empty, we entered; and there settled to recover our sense and make plans.

It was now nearly dusk, and we proposed to remain hid where we were till next day. Then, perchance, the cavalcade would have moved on; and we would be free to emerge, perhaps steal some clothes from somewhere, and so make our way to the coast as Frenchmen.

So we settled, making beds of some straw and loose bracken we found in a loft. And were dosing happily into slumber when I heard (heaven help me!) a sound associated forever with the dreadful moment of our capture on the beach at Lytchett.

It was the sound of whistling. And it was the sound of the little air by Haydn which Abershaw had so often played to us!

The door of our loft creaked open, a long thin pencil of light traversing the room as it did so, from a lantern held outside.

By the light of the lantern we saw, regarding us quietly, the tall and fearful shape of our arch-enemy himself; smiling, as always.

"You but serve, my friends," he remarked, "—you but serve to illustrate the value of some of my activities. I have worked hard to convince the authorities, who are conservative in their outlook, that I am not only playing with toys. You stand as living proof of my success—I may some day show you to my beloved First Consul himself as such; he, I know, *is* interested in my proposals."

As he spoke, he was pointing upwards with the long naked sabre he held in his hand.

"The balloon!" gasped Butterfield. "Deuce take it! —the balloon! I never thought of it!—and by George I've actually been up in balloons myself in England!"

"Precisely, Lieutenant. The balloon. It was on the point of coming down when you made your bid at escape. But before it did, the officers in it, engaged in any case in scanning the country with glasses, perceived you entering this place of shelter. They communicated the information to me when they descended. . . . I warrant you looked back, my friends, as you ran—all escaping men look *back*. But you did not think to look *up*."

He advanced towards us with the men who followed him. We had time, only time to conceal in a crack in the rotting wall behind us the two packages Mignonne had prepared—else her complicity might have been discovered. Then we rose to fresh captivity.

"I do not think you will escape again so easily," continued Blackadder. "To-morrow we should be at the place where all along I have designed to set you. I shall leave you there, my friends, until certain necessary business has been performed. Then—" and he peered close to my eyes, and gripped my arm as in a vice, "—then, M. le Chevalier, we shall see—we shall see!"

The old mesmeric look was in his eyes. They glinted yellow in the lantern light.

"You are too valuable to lose, de Rohan—too valuable to lose," he whispered. And a chill went through and through me at the close glimpse of his white face, his long sharp bared teeth.

V: PRISON

Late next evening we encamped at a place named Tacoignières. Near it was a large prison used for English prisoners of war. Here, without more ado, we were incarcerated. And thus we stayed close-guarded for many, many weary months.

CHAPTER THE SECOND

I: THE MONTHS PASS BY

THE PRISON at Tacoignières was a place of terror, which I do not care to remember.

The part of the fortress in which we ourselves were confined was called *La Grosse Tête*. It was a place of many corridors, ill-lit and of evil smell. We three—Tom, Butterfield and I—were conducted to a small cell or dungeon in one of these corridors, which we were to share. The other men—Blue Nose and the seamen—were taken to a large common room lower down, in the very earth itself; where they consorted with some Corsican deserters from the French army and some low fellows of our own forces who had been taken in recent fighting.

We were given bad food, were permitted very little air; and for the most part moped haplessly through the days in a weary dream.

The prison guards were gross cruel fellows—late criminals themselves, as we supposed. They sought every opportunity to punish us. Once Butterfield spoke to one of them in his forthright way and was at once conveyed to a deep oubliette, far below the surface of the ground; and there remained for some ten days on black bread and water. When he emerged he was thin and weak—a shadow of his rubicund self. But his gallant spirit remained undamped.

Later, things grew a little easier. Blackadder, it seemed, had gone on to Paris on business connected with his spying activities, leaving Kabal and McGuffie encamped in a permanent military village outside the walls of the fortress. Frequently McGuffie came to see us. It was at this time that, strangely, our friendship with him began. He was a despicable renegade, an acknowledged spy and enemy of his own country; but there was something likeable in the man, and his frequent bouts of remorse made us hope that some day he would revoke and come into the fold again.

Kabal came, too, at intervals—presumably to observe on Blackadder's behalf that we were safely and staunchly restrained from any further escape attempts. And although there was nothing in any degree likeable about *him*, he still occasionally unbent and stayed talking with us. It was at this time, from these two, that we learned something of Blackadder's past history —I the more particularly pressing for information, to find what the connection between us from the past might be.

"You say he was an ardent Revolutionary?" said I.

"Indeed," replied Louis Kabal. "He and I were first associated then. He was implacable—a believer in the strongest doctrines of destruction."

"Ah! Against any particular family?"

"Against all aristocrats."

"Any family more than any other?"

"None."

And so I had to leave it—but all the time, at the back of my mind, there lingered that *phrase*, that phrase or name which I felt certain contained the secret of all. . . .

Only once, in all the long months, did we see the master-spy himself. He came into our cell one winter's night in the start of the year 1804. For a long moment he regarded us.

"You wear well," he said with a sneer.

"Devil take you, sir," exploded Butterfield, "—we wear well because we are English! We will not give you the satisfaction of seeing us weaken."

"As you say, Lieutenant. Your country, however, is in no position to do likewise."

"What do you mean, confound you?"

"That the war is unlikely to last, Lieutenant. On all sides we gain on you—France conquers. We destroy you on sea and land. Moreover, your people know it."

"How?"

"I have been into England again myself, Lieutenant, since our last sight of each other. I stayed for some months in London—oh, not as Abershaw this time, nor yet as Blackadder. I had a new disguise which will not be specified. I found what I had hoped to find. Panic spreads everywhere—your people live in a constant terror of invasion. They feel themselves doomed—as indeed they are."

"I refuse to believe it, sir!"

"No doubt, no doubt. I but tell you the truth. If you believe it or not is no concern to me. . . ."

He turned abruptly to me.

"As for you, de Rohan—I was not able to do one of

the things I intended to do in England—I had not time for that. It can wait, however—there is no haste for it. But I did at least send a message on your behalf."

"A message?"

"To your respected relative—your grandfather. He was, as you may fancy, prostrate after your . . . disappearance, shall I call it?"

I could have risen to strike him, weak as I was. He sneered abominably.

"I simply informed him—through an agent, of course, for I could not go myself—I simply informed him. . . ."

He hesitated tantalisingly. I said nothing, but was trembling in anxiety. It was Butterfield who burst out:

" 'Fore God, man, are you the devil himself? What did you tell this boy's grandfather?"

"Only that he was well, Lieutenant," said the other smoothly. "Only that he was alive and well! It was the least I could do, I think—in view of his great anxiety."

I stared. How could I read the twisted motives of the man before me? I recalled, foolishly and irrelevantly, the strange occasion when, in the longboat out to the *Manon*, he had given Tom and me a slice of shortcake. But Blackadder was going on; and his voice was its low evil menace again;

"Besides—besides, M. le petit Chevalier, I had a reason —a private one—for wanting the old gentleman to know just that—that you were alive and well. The reason will grow apparent in due course, no doubt. Gentlemen, your servant!"

And he went, with a sweep of his black cloak; and the door of our cell swung to with a great clang behind him.

II: THE TUNNEL

Do not imagine that we did not think longingly and continuously of escape. In all the long weary months of our imprisonment in the fortress, we brooded incessantly on ways and means.

And at last it seemed that a plan was possible. As before, it was Mignonne who helped us; and it came about thus:

She had, of course, at the outset of our term of imprisonment, gone on to Paris with her mother to see her father in the barrack there. They had had together a brief spell of happiness. But then had arisen a set of circumstances which completely confirmed Mignonne in her hatred of Napoleon.

Very briefly (for in a sense it is outside my main story—is indeed a whole separate story on its own account which I may some day persuade my wife to write down*)—very briefly what happened was this:

Mignonne's father, de Barbaroux, was no ordinary man. He was of Breton fisher-folk stock, of course, but was a studious and thoughtful fellow from all accounts, something of a poet. At the outset of Napoleon's career, he had hailed the remarkable Corsican with some fervour as a man likely to weld together the scattered strength of his beloved France after the

* Mignonne de Barbaroux, I am happy to say, honoured me by becoming Mrs. Henry Rowan some few years after the end of our adventure. —H.R.

Revolution. But gradually, as he had seen Bonaparte's ambition grow, he had formed the slow conclusion that far from being an angel, Napoleon was something of a monster—who would end by destroying France instead of saving her.

He had joined the First Consul's forces towards the end of the first phase of our war with him—in the days when he still believed the man was a saint. He was made a sergeant in 1800, and was by the time of our own tale a permanent official in the barrack at Paris.

All the time, however, his secret thoughts were changing him from a man who believed in Napoleon to a man who hated and wished to destroy him.

In this impasse he was approached by a group of Frenchmen who were building a conspiracy to assassinate the First Consul. This huge project had been planned in England, by a group of émigrés from the old Revolution. De Barbaroux joined the conspirators and worked for the death of Bonaparte—which, as he now believed, was the only thing that could save France.

Early in 1804 the conspiracy was discovered. Napoleon believed that the leader of it was the young Duke of Enghien. He had him arrested and taken to Paris. He was excuted. In the consequent investigation the names of several more of the conspirators came to light. Among them was de Barbaroux.

Mignonne had the bitter mortification of seeing her own father executed in public as a traitor in March of 1804. Her mother, who had been ailing for some time, was shattered by the cruel tragedy; and died about a month later.

In the extremity of her suffering, Mignonne had now one thought and one thought only: to escape from France herself—to forget all allegiance to the tyrant whom all along she had secretly hated and who now had deprived her of a father. And matters were made worse in the consideration that the man who had brought about the overthrow of the Duke of Enghien and his followers—who had unearthed the details of the assassination plot in the course of his recent visit to England, was none other than our own arch-enemy—Blackadder!

Mignonne travelled alone from Paris to Tacoignières. In her hatred for Blackadder, her sympathy for us, she was determined to do all she could to help us to escape, so that she could come to England with us.

She succeeded in establishing herself in the camp outside the fortress walls—represented herself to the authorities there as an orphan child devoted to the cause of the Grand Army. They, knowing nothing of her antecedents (Blackadder, the only man who might have suspected anything deeper in her, was off on another expedition at the time), gave her a menial position in the camp laundry—which she gladly took.

She cultivated a friendship with McGuffie—who, in his sentimental way, had always liked "the bonnie wee lass," as he called her. And thus, in the end, she was able to get permission to visit us occasionally in the fortress.

At the outset, McGuffie or Kabal always accompanied

her on these visits, which were represented as being merely social—she bringing us occasional dainties of food from outside and so on. But latterly she so convinced the guards of her goodwill that she was permitted to come to see us quite frequently unattended; and it was from now that I must date the serious building of our plan of escape.

It was, no less, a scheme to dig a long tunnel from a corner of one of the dungeons in *La Grosse Tête* right outside the walls of the Fortress of Tacoignières itself!

III: WE DIG

I must briefly describe something of the geography of the fortress.

It was built atop a steep hill—had been, in the old days, a castle reared and fortified there against attack.

The prison was, as it were, in several "layers." The main corridors and cells were on ground level. Below that, in the cellars, so to say, were larger cells for the more common sort of prisoners (it was in one of these large unhealthy rooms that old Blue Nose and his companions were incarcerated).

Below that again were several large dungeons, quite devoid of light, which were used for punishment purposes. It was in one of these that Butterfield had once been imprisoned for insulting one of the guards.

But because the fortress stood on the steep-sloping hill it follows that although these dungeons were well under ground, they were still comparatively accessible to the open *sideways*. The following crude sketch will show exactly what I mean:

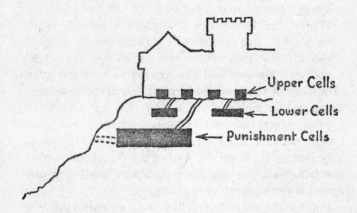

Our plan, in its essence, was this: We would contrive to create a set of circumstances where each one of us would be due for punishment. We would, we hoped, then be placed in one of the deep dungeons, and left comparatively alone; and while there we would dig and burrow *horizontally*; and so emerge into the fresh free air of the hillside.

From now on, Mignonne resolutely set out to smuggle into us various tools and parts of tools which we were able to conceal on our persons; thus a small pick-axe came in in a pie she brought us one day—or rather the head of it did; the handle came in another day inside a woollen stocking she had knitted for our winter comfort. The tools were small enough, heaven knows (had they been larger it would have been impossible for us to conceal them); but we calculated that they would serve our purpose—if we worked determinedly enough at our digging.

Within the fortress we contrived a meeting with Blue Nose (it was occasionally possible for us to do so when all the prisoners were on a working party together). We outlined the scheme to him and gave him some of the tools for himself and his companions, Wasp and Driffield.

From Mignonne—who was indispensable—we got a rough plan of the fortress, so that we would know how best to dig from the wall of the dungeon. And at last, when all was ready, we set about contriving our removal to the scene of our attempt.

For Lieutenant Butterfield it was an easy matter—he was notorious for his choleric temper against the guards; it merely was necessary for him to insult one of them, and presto! he, the first of us, was comfortably (or rather uncomfortably) installed, his digging weapon, a small adze in two parts, safely concealed on his person.

Blue Nose and the others had little difficulty either: grouped as they were among the deserters, they were regarded as mere rascals whom it was almost a duty (and certainly a pleasure) for the guards to punish. They simply staged a brawl one evening—and, after a brief inquiry in which they took care to let it be seen that they were the ringleaders, they too were cast into the huge, dank, punishment dungeon.

Tom and myself found it more difficult. We were

noted for our "good" behaviour!—meaning no more than that we had always, mainly out of contempt for the ruffians in charge of us, avoided crossing them in any way.

There was one man, however, a thin melancholy wretch named Braque, who disliked us and lost no opportunity to give us extra menial work to do. It was this fellow's aim to sneak continuously round us in the hope that he would be able to trap us in some forbidden conduct; he seemed inspired in all his dealings with his fellow-mortals by an unreasoning spiteful malice.

For some time this man Braque had been transferred to another part of the prison; but not long after Butterfield's "descent" to the oubliette, he came back to *La Grosse Tête*. We were overjoyed!—but naturally gave no sign to this effect.

Tom and I contrived things one day so that when Braque was on his rounds we were arguing furiously in our cell—as if quarrelling. As we talked we heard his footsteps coming along the corridor and stealthily stopping outside to overhear what we were saying. At a sign from me, Tom at once began to vilify this fellow Braque—and I, as it were, stopped my quarrel with him to agree that he was indeed "a low and filthy blackguard, that I was sorry he had ever come back to *La Grosse Tête*, etc."

It was an offence to malign a guard; and with an expression of unholy glee Braque swung open the door of our cell and confronted us.

We appeared to be disconcerted for a moment; then,

as it were carried away still by our passion, we insulted him openly to his face when he challenged us with having spoken against him.

We were conveyed before the *Marechal de Logis*; accused by Braque; and instantly sentenced (to our secret delight) to "six days in the main oubliette on black bread and water."

Thus we joined our friends at last, in the dark depths; and began to dig—to dig and dig and dig! . . .

IV: MADNESS

Butterfield and the others had already succeeded in penetrating some distance into the soil and rock which lay beyond the wall of the oubliette.

The most difficult part of the operation had been to open the wall itself, which was of hard flinty stone. But Blue Nose, a man of great strength for all his quiet manner, succeeded at last in prising away some of the mortar, so making a start to our tunnel. The loosened stones were piled close at hand; and when a spell of digging in the tunnel itself was over, or during those periods when our food was brought to us by the dungeon guards, the surface of the wall was built up again with them, so that it seemed to an observer in the dim lantern light that comprised the only illumination when we were visited, that all was as it should be. The excavated earth was smeared thinly and evenly over the floor of the huge cell and stamped down into the parts of it which were not paved; and so there were no traces of our activites.

We worked in turns, stopping only when we had to. The labour was gruelling—we were all weak from our long term of imprisonment—weaker still from the ill nourishment we now got of black bread and water.

With us, in the cell, was an old fellow who had been in the oubliette for many, many months — a deserter from the Grand Army. He had killed a fellow prisoner in a fit of insanity, and had been in solitary confinement in the huge damp loathsome den ever since.

It was our terror that this crazed old fellow would betray us—as indeed in the end he did. But throughout our period of digging at least he stayed quiet, mumbling incessantly in a dark corner, singing snatches of weird songs, sometimes weeping in a remorse for the comrade he had killed.

We worked on and on. Our food was brought to us once a day by two guards, who also scanned each one of us closely with upheld lanterns to see how we fared. On these visits we feigned great weakness of spirit—lay back with lack-lustre eyes and pretended the utmost depression. They would smile and joke with each other as they saw the straits we were in, and so depart; and the moment they were gone we would spring to life in the nervous fever of hope that inspired us, open up the hole in the wall and crawl along the lengthening tunnel to dig further and yet further.

One of us always kept a watch at the grill of the door of the cell, lest one of the guards should surprise us with an unaccustomed visit. And indeed on one occasion we were so surprised—and it nearly led to disaster.

Tom was at the grill, the seaman Wasp at the end of the tunnel, Blue Nose and Butterfield at the wall, fetching back the handfuls of excavated earth Wasp passed to them. Suddenly Tom gave a low whistle, agreed between us as a signal; and ran over to tell us that he could hear footsteps descending the long dank corridor to the oubliette.

There was no other thing for it but to seal up the wall. We hastily pushed into the aperture the little heaps of newly excavated earth and piled up the stones, leaving Wasp inside.

Then rapidly we took up our positions—Blue Nose reclining back upon the very stones that covered the entrance to the tunnel. And with admirable presence of mind the old seaman huddled up a pile of blankets in the shadow by his side to represent, in the dim light, a reclining human form, so that our number would seem complete.

The door opened and one of the guards came in. He was grumbling sullenly. Behind him, of all men, was McGuffie.

"Well, well," said the latter, advancing, and speaking in his uncouth dialect: "Well, well, this is the way o't, is it! Ye're a sorry sight the lot o' ye. Aye in trouble you laddies—can ye no' behave yoursel's?"

"We have little alternative but to behave ourselves, as you put it," said Butterfield shortly.

"True enough, true enough. They tellt me ye were a' down here a few days syne, but they wouldnae let me come to see ye. I'm here now just for a moment or two—it was his Nainsel was able to arrange it."

(This expression, "his Nainsel," meaning in the Scots tongue "his own self," was a phrase McGuffie occasionally used to refer to his Master—Blackadder.)

"It was just, ye see, that I was to have a look at ye a', to see how ye were," the Scot went on; "and to let ye have a wee bit message frae him, Maister Harry," (which was how he always referred to me).

"A message?"

"Aye. He's been off on business, ye ken, but he sent word I was to come in to see ye and to tell ye he was coming back the morn."

"To-morrow?"

"Aye, the morn. And I was to be sure to let ye know that he had something important to tell ye—some kind o' surprise, like."

"A surprise? What surprise?"

"Oh, ye have me there! I wouldnae ken. His Nainsel doesnae tell me everything. But ye may be sure it's something big—he doesnae do things on the wee scale does yon yin."

All this time the guard was standing back with the lantern held high, scanning us all. Suddenly, he nodded suspiciously to the bundle of blankets on the floor beside Blue Nose.

"What is wrong with that prisoner?" he demanded angrily.

The old seaman stared blankly. The guard, of course, spoke in French. It was Butterfield, who had a smattering of the language, who answered:

"He is ill," said he gruffly. "He lies and sleeps all day. *Malade, malade*—" (then, in English, his French running out)—"*ill*, confound it!"

The guard for a moment seemed as if he would stir the bundle with his foot; but at this moment the old maniac in his corner began to howl and weep as he so often did.

"Marcel," he cried, "oh, Marcel—Marcel! I didn't mean it, Marcel—I never meant it—never, never!"

"Mercy on us!" cried McGuffie. "What's that? Who's old girny there?"

"Tach, it is nothing, monsieur," said the guard. "Only old Bouvard. He murdered his comrade Marcel a year ago, and thinks his ghost lives here in the dungeon with him." He chuckled. "We permit him to stay on as an added pleasure to the other rogues who might be sent here. They come to believe in Marcel's ghost too—like Bouvard they wish he would go away, and yet also that he would not go away, for even a ghost can be company for a man in the oubliette of *La Grosse Tête*!"

"D'ye tell me that!" said McGuffie. "Well, well— it's a while ere I'd be exactly joco at the thought o' a ghost for company. Still, every man to his taste, as the old wife said when she kissed the cow. We'd better haud away, I suppose—cannae say I exactly like the air down here."

He turned, the guard with him, the reclining figure of "Wasp" forgotten. McGuffie turned to me for a last word:

"I daresay ye'll hear more the morn," he said. "His

Nainsel will be here wi' this 'surprise' o' his, whatever it may be. Man, ye'd think he was bringing ye a birthday present or something, eh?"

"I care nothing for him or his surprise," said I, "—whatever it might be."

"I wouldnae be too sure o' that. He's a sly one yon. Depend on it he's got something up his sleeve. He wouldnae send me here wi' a silly message like that if it wasnae *for* something. Oh, he's cunning—cunning! Like his name—a kind o' serpent. That's what the Maister is—a kind o' black serpent!—a viper, sir."

A moment later he was gone, the guard with him. I lay staring after him. For his last remark had brought all into mind at last!—I recalled, in one strange flash, everything I had tried to remember of Blackadder since ever he had spoken to me in the hold of the *Manon*.

A serpent! A black serpent! A viper! And I recollected—I recollected——

But there was no time for further thought. Blue Nose was tearing at the stones of the wall. A moment later Wasp crawled exhaustedly out of the tunnel. He was on the point of collapse. If the guard and McGuffie had lingered a moment longer, he would have fainted from the foul still air in the tunnel.

And with the approaching visit of Blackadder it was essential that we should push ahead with all our might. It was unlikely that our work on the tunnel would escape *his* eagle eye—to say nothing of the fact that if he had something to say to me I would probably be removed from the dungeon altogether. . . .

Fortunately, only a few feet remained to be dug; and

before another hour had elapsed we had scraped them away: a small circle of daylight appeared before us as we broke gently through the outer crust.

Our arrangement with Mignonne was very simple. From the plan of the tunnel we had made we knew fairly exactly where it would break on the hillside. Every morning and afternoon, Mignonne was to visit that spot. When we broke crust we were to thrust through a note to her, which she would find on one of these visits. This would let her know that we were now ready for the final break. She would thrust back a little note to us telling us when to make the attempt and letting us know that she would be waiting for us at the foot of the slope.

We now thrust our note through—with an added warning to her that it was essential we should break that very night.

Within another hour the note had been taken and another set in its place.

"Very well—to-night," it said. "An hour after dusk. . . ."

V: DEATH

Thus all was ready at last.

We took it in turns to crouch at the end of the tunnel, watching the little circle of light. As it faded to dusk we knew we could calculate an hour with reasonable accuracy.

The problem was that it was usually an hour after dusk when our food came in. And yet on reflection it was better so: we would make the break immediately the guards were gone—then it would be a long twenty-four hours before our departure was discovered.

We were worried about the old lunatic, Bouvard. Should we take him with us? Yet he crouched incessantly in his corner—it seemed unlikely that he would even know what we were about. We decided to leave him.

The guards came. They gave us our dole of food and checked our numbers. They went.

On the instant, Blue Nose and Driffield tore down the barricade of stones. One by one we crept forward into the tunnel, Wasp in the front. He immediately set about scraping the last thin crust of earth away.

And then, behind us there broke out the most appalling commotion! Bouvard!

"Marcel!" he howled. "Marcel! Do not leave me—oh, never leave me! Do not go through the tunnel with them, Marcel!—oh, never leave me, never, never, never!"

In his insanity he thought that the ghost of his murdered friend—his only company in all the long months of confiement—proposed to depart with us through the tunnel!

The din he created was unbelievable—worse than anything we had heard from him before. It was impossible for the guards not to hear it.

And indeed, even as we crouched there, we were aware of their rushing footsteps back down the long corridor.

"Deuce take it!" bellowed Butterfield. "We're lost, men—we're lost!"

"No, sir," said Blue Nose calmly. "Not yet! Wasp, are you through?"

"Through!" cried Wasp. "Through it is, shipmate!"

"Now heaven be praised," said Blue Nose, still in his calm undistrubed tones.

And we thrust forward, blindly, into the night—the fresh air a tonic in our faces after the enclosed foulness of the dungeon.

But behind us Bouvard still screamed. And the guards were in the cell. And the tunnel was discovered.

We rushed forward. The slope upon which we found ourselves was steep in the extreme, all dotted over with little bushes and potholes. With Tom at my side I went scrambling down—down and down, stumbling and tumbling, rolling, catching at twigs until my hands bled.

Above us were the guards. They had reached the exit to the tunnel and were firing blindly after us. But the night was pitch and they could see nothing.

Yet one of their shots found a billet, alas. At the moment when we reached the foot of the incline there was a great high cry from little Wasp.

"I'm done," he screamed in an agony. "Oh, my heart, my heart! Ah, Johnny Corinth*—Johnny, Handsome Johnny!"

He rolled over and over.

* His shipmate who had died aboard the *Manon*—Ed.

Simultaneously I heard the frightened voice of Mignonne from the darkness.

"Oh, Tom—Harry—are you safe?—are you safe?"

"All safe," I whispered, taking her hand.

Blue Nose loomed in the darkness.

"He is dead," he said solemnly, "Jo Wasp is dead. A shot in the heart. . . ."

We were by this time all assembled. Above us, the musket fire still went on. We turned to run, Mignonne guiding us in the way she had planned. But as we did so there was a moaning from the second seaman, Driffield.

"My leg—I sprained my leg coming down. I can't do it, sir. Leave me—go on alone!"

"Confound it, man, you must do it!" exclaimed Butterfield.

"No, sir. It is broken, I think. Go on, your honour—*go on!*"

There was no other thing for it. We left him lying—to what fate thereafter we never fully learned. The rest of us made into the night with what speed we could; and in a short while the sound of the firing died away behind us.

We were thus in the open once more. The following: Myself, Tom, Butterfield, Blue Nose and Mignonne.

CHAPTER THE THIRD

I: OUR FLIGHT ACROSS FRANCE

I WILL not weary you with a long recital of our adventures after we left Tacoignières. They have been dealt with in detail elsewhere*; to recapitulate upon them would be merely to chew over an old cud.

It will suffice for the present to say that we were some months on the road, and that in the course of them we suffered much—were frequently upon the point of discovery; and even, on occasions, at the height of our weariness, contemplated giving ourselves up.

Our aim was to get to the coast of Normandy. At Cherbourg, Mignonne had a cousin upon whom, she felt certain, we might rely for help. It was possible that at least we could obtain a small boat there and so beat across the Channel for home.

Meantime, the problem was to reach there!

In the week of our confinement in the dungeon, Mignonne had been making a host of practical arrangements. At a point some distance to the north of the fortress she had discovered a deep cave in a hillside. To this, she had conveyed supplies of food and (suffi-

---

* See *The Narrative of an Escape from a French Prison in the Years* 1804 *and* 1805 by Admiral Sir Thomas Cathro, printed in *The Naval Chronicle* in the year 1840. H.R.

cient for our whole party) French peasant costumes. She had also contrived to lay in a small store of money; and a little old-style pistol—which latter, by common consent, was handed over to Lieutenant Butterfield.

For the cave we made the first night; and lay there for three days, feeling secure in it. Once, and once only, looking out, did we see anything like a search party—a little group of *gens-d'armes* afar off. But they passed a good three-quarter mile away from us. We did not venture much from the cave itself in that early part—and if we did, remembering the lesson of the balloon, we kept an eye upon the sky!

Eventually, when we were tolerably certain that the first heat of any chase would have died, we sallied forth; and began our journey, making north-west.

We posed as French peasants—Butterfield and Blue Nose taking care to observe absolute silence if we encountered anyone. All talking was left to Mignonne and myself. If questioned too closely we had a tale of being members of a troop of travelling players heading northwards to join our main company, which was then to proceed towards Boulogne for the entertainment of the troops gathered there by Bonaparte for the proposed invasion of Britain. This fiction accounted admirably for any seeming eccentricity of our behaviour and appearance!

There were many narrow escapes. Once we were challenged by a group of *gens-d'armes* and asked to show our papers. We had, of course, none; and things might have gone badly indeed if we had not on Mignonne's suggestion parted with some of our little store of money to the Captain of the group; and so were allowed to pass.

Another time there was continuous rain for some four or five days on end. We were much exposed, and in our already weakened condition were close to despair in the constant discomfort of our soaked clothes. Butterfield was lame from the enforced walking, and old Blue Nose sickened of a fever. We lay with him in a covert in some woods for many hours, he urging us always to go on and leave him, Butterfield and we others refusing.

But somehow, through these and other hardships, we won through. We reached the coast at a place named Formigny; and from there proposed to work by easy stages to Cherbourg itself.

And all the time—although we did not then know it—we were indeed being pursued; and by no other a person than Blackadder himself. Let me briefly here recount his movements, as they were later represented to us by the ever-informative McGuffie.

II: THE PURSUIT (ACCORDING TO HABBAKUK McGUFFIE)

Man, man (said McGuffie) but the Maister was in a rage yon time! When he came back frae Paris and found ye had escaped again he was like a man possessed. I was fair fliggit! *

The worst o' it was that he had that famous surprise for ye, d'y'see—and I'll no' deny it was a surprise to

* Frightened.

me too when I saw what it was. Holy mackerel, the man was no' canny—no' canny! I didnae ken how he had done it, but somehow he had—oh, he was as cunning as the Sairpint his Nainsel was!—as cunning as the Sairpint!

Anyways, there he was, the day after ye went oot through that tunnel o' yours, and he was ragin' back and forth like a lion. He had the twa guards up that had been supposed to look after ye and, the pair o' them were like men demented in front o' him. There was one o' them turned on him and said he couldnae help it if ye had been digging away—how was he to know?—and the Maister ups wi' his riding whip and flings him full across the face wi' it; and the man went greetin' in a corner and a big red mark on his cheek like the brand o' the very Deil.

After that his Nainsel has a chat wi' the man wi' the broken leg ye had to leave behind. He was at the ploy o' finding out what wey ye had gone, d'y'see; but this man o' yours, Driffield, said he didnae ken.

"Ye do ken," says the Maister (no in the braid Scots, of course—this is just the way I'm telling it.)

"I dinnae," says Driffield.

"Aweel, we'll see," says his Nainsel. "We'll just see!"

And he's for torturing him on the spot, d'y'see. But up speaks the Governor o' the Prison.

"Na, na, sir," he pipes. "We'll have nane o' that. I ken ye're a powerful-like body, Mossoor Blackadder, and maybe ye'll be able to get me into trouble for no' doing just what ye tell me. But I dinnae like torture, and I'm the Marechal o' this Prison, sir, and as long as this man Driffield is in my care he'll no be subjectit to anything like that. He's an escapit prisoner and of course he'll be punished for that, but in my way, sir, and no' yours."

And there it just had to rest. The auld Governor was right—it was up to him to say what was to happen to Driffield. He was no a bad old soul that Governor; I wouldnae have been very well-pleased mysel' if the Maister had had his way wi' Driffield. I canna thole torture.

Anyway, Driffield wouldnae speak—and I'm no' sure in any case that he did ken what wey ye were due to go when ye escaped.* He was taken away and I've no doubt he was punished for trying to get out; but at least he wasnae tortured. What did happen to him I just dinnae ken.

Well, his Nainsel went ravin' on at me and Kabal after that—kind o' blaming *us*! As if we could have helped it!

And next, he gets out search parties for ye—but wi' one thing and another it was some days before he could get this under way. He had dogs out, but they never picked up the scent. And he had one o' his balloons up—went up in it himsel' and glowered ower all the countryside like an old hawk. But there was no sign o' ye.

At last, in comes Kabal. He had found a cave up north somewhere, and there were your prison clothes

* This was perfectly true; none of us knew till we met Mignonne what direction of escape she had planned for us. H.R.

and all. The Maister had guessed that ye would be headin' north, of course, so as to get to the coast, and had been concentrating all round that way. But the find o' the cave gave us a starting place at least, so there we were.

For a while we cast round among a' the folk in that part, in the hope ye'd been seen. We didnae ken what ye were dressed like now, o' course, but we kent what ye looked like at least, and so we speired here and there and gave out your descriptions.

And at last, maybe a week or ten days after ye had gone, we came on an auld body that remembered ye and the way ye were headin'. He tellt us there was a bit lassie wi' ye, and that was a new one on us; but suddenly I minded wee Mignonne and that I hadnae seen her aboot the camp since ye had gone; and so I kent it must be her.

Off we went, me and Kabal and his Nainsel. Man, ye led us a dance! There were times when I thocht his Nainsel would explode like a bomb when we lost the trail o' ye and had to cast about to try to pick it up again! He sat there on that black horse o' his the very picture o' Auld Clootie himsel'*; and one time when I ventured a bit word or two o' suggestion and consolation like, he was round on me like a warlock wi' his sword out.

"McGuffie," says he (I could never get him to call me Habbie, which is what I like to be called, or even Habbakuk, if ye must gang the whole way)— "McGuffie," says he, "if ye dinnae keep that—(some-

* The Devil.

thing something something) tongue o' yours quiet, I'll rip ye open so I will, ye—(something something something) auld blether! "

"Harsh words, Maister," says I.

"Aye—and they'll be followed by harsh deeds," says he. "Mind, I'm telling you, McGuffie!—I mean it! "

And there was a kind o' glint in yon black eyes o' his that made me think he mebbe did mean it this time. So I kept kind o' quiet for a while after that—though it was hard, man—oh, it was hard, hard, hard! and me just keen for a bit friendly word wi' folk whiles. . . .

At last, the time came when his Nainsel had to leave us and go back to his place near Paris that was his headquarters them days. He made Kabal and me swear we'd never give up till we found ye. And off he gallops —back to that *surprise* he had for ye, and that ye ken all about by now, of course.

Well, Louis and I went on and on. We met in wi' some folk that had seen ye at Caen. And we picked up too wi' one or two o' they *jenns darmies* fellows, so that there would be enough o' us to tackle ye if we did succeed in gettin' hold o' ye. And of course as ye know, Maister Harry—as ye know——

*III: I RESUME IN MY OWN WORDS; AND
RELATE HOW WE WERE RETAKEN; AND
HOW I LEARNED AT LAST THE NATURE
OF BLACKADDER'S "SURPRISE"*

—of course, as we knew indeed, we were re-arrested.

It fell thus (and in telling it I move towards the end of this my present contribution to the narrative:)

We had reached Cherbourg. We lay for a while well outside the town, concealed in a tumbledown hut on a deserted stretch of beach.

Blue Nose was by this time a desperately sick man. His normally bluff constitution had suffered terribly in the long forced marches on land we had been forced to make. He had never shaken off his fever—most nights, when we set up to rest, he went into a kind of delirium and raved of his days aboard the old *Hawk*. Sometimes he fancied himself in older days still, when he had sailed with Admiral Nelson. He had been with him during the unsuccessful attempt to capture Teneriffe—had been one of the crew of the very boat which had carried the great Admiral to the Mole and in which he had been standing when he received the wound which was to cost him his arm.

"Hold hard, sir!" he cried in his delirium, imagining himself present again at that scene of terrible slaughter. "Ah, he falls—he falls! God keep him!"

Then he supposed himself the Admiral himself for a moment; and cried out:

"I am shot through the arm—I am a dead man!..."

And an instant later he fancied himself at the terrible scene in the *Thesus* when the amputation of the shattered limb took place.

"The knife," he cried, "—ah, the cold knife! . . ." (And yet as we know, no word of such complaint had ever passed our beloved Admiral's own lips: it was possible indeed that those who were there, like Blue Nose, had felt the pain in an excruciation of sympathy for their beloved leader, and so cried out at the touch of the knife as he did not. . . .)

All this went forth that last night of our freedom in the little deserted hut on the foreshore near Cherbourg. We others were wearied too with our long exposure and hardship—Butterfield a martyr to the great raw wounds in his feet, to which the very leather of his boots had congealed. But we did what we might to comfort poor Blue Nose—none more than Butterfield himself, who wiped the hot brow with a damp rag, who murmured words of comfort and compassion—he who was so brusque, so bold and forthright. Ah, George Butterfield! You were a man, you were a man! God bless your gallant memory! . . .

It was for Mignonne we waited. She had gone forward alone into the town, to make contact with her cousin from whom we hoped for a boat. At last she came, wearied from the long walk and soaked in a storm of rain which had blown up outside. She stood for a moment by the broken doorway, her lips trembling; and we knew from her expression before she spoke that she had been disappointed.

"He is gone," she said. "My cousin has gone! He

is no longer in the town. He left a few weeks ago—he was conscripted to join the Grand Army. . . ."

She advanced towards us. And behind her the door swung open. We thought for a moment that it moved in a gust of the wind. But as I rose to close and secure it, it opened wider; and in its rotting frame were the figures of Louis Kabal and McGuffie—the former momentarily with something in him of the evil triumph of his master, Blackadder.

"We meet again, gentlemen," he said—and the very tones of his voice seemed to echo the thin edginess of those of his master. Never indeed was the whole dark spirit of a man so present at a scene in which he did not bodily take part. "We meet again, gentlemen— and " (with a bow) "and mademoiselle. . . . We were loath to lose your excellent company and so took the liberty of following you—guided, indeed, by the hurrying figure of yourself, mademoiselle, whom we saw leaving Cherbourg at the very moment we were about to enter it. For which our everlasting thanks."

"Hech, hech," said McGuffie, also entering. "Ye've led us a dance, the crowd o' ye—a bonny dance, sirs! And on a night like this forbye! Och, man—ye might ' a ' chosen better weather! "

Behind them, crowding into the hut with them, were some half-dozen *gens-d'armes*. To have attempted resistance would have been mere folly.

And so, in the utmost bitterness of spirit, we went back. Our captors took us forward into Cherbourg first, where they commandeered a rough carriage. In it we travelled for many weary days in a silence of despair towards Paris, Kabal and McGuffie riding beside us, the *gens-d'armes* trotting in the rear with arms all ready.

The one small consolation was that in the comparative comfort of the journey, Blue Nose recovered some of his health—as did Butterfield. Yet rested in body though we were, in spirit we were utterly broken. To have failed—to have failed again; and this time with success so close (for we could somehow have found another boat at Cherbourg—at the worst would have stolen one). . . .

We headed north of the city. Where we were being taken we did not know; but it was not, at least, back to Tacoignières.

At last, on a bright chill morning of early autumn, we swung with our little equipage through the ancient mouldering gates of a great house. For a while I had had a sense (it could *only* have been a sense, transmitted into me in some mysterious way beyond comprehension) that I was in a familiar place. And as we passed under the canopy of the great gateway, and I saw above me on the lichened stone an emblem I knew so well, I rose up to my feet in the cart there and cried:

"Rohan!   Rohan!   Rohan-Soubise!"

It was indeed: the ancient house of our line; where I had been born and from which we all had fled so many years before.

In a bewilderment I scanned the house itself as we approached it—familiar from a thousand descriptions I had heard from my grandfather, a hundred drawings and engravings which he had collected and which reposed at our little house so far away at Lytchett.

We were hurried from the cart and pushed forward by Kabal up the great winding stairway to the main door. All round us, in the grounds, were tents and cabins, the place being used now, it seemed as some kind of temporary military barrack. Abstractedly, as I cast my eyes around the sad scene (and they were misty in the swell of my emotion) I saw one of Blackadder's great observation balloons, half-inflated, rising above a cluster of bushes like a huge blind head, nodding to and fro in the breeze.

We were pushed forward into the hallway—farther, into a vast bare room that once had been, as I knew, the library.

In the centre of it, seated at a table, a baleful figure in the gloom, was the Master-spy himself. He rose to his full gaunt evil height at our approach, his face a twist of malice and wicked pleasure.

"Welcome," he whispered, his voice an echo round all the bare walls. "Welcome, my friends! To you in particular, M. le petit Chevalier! Welcome ... home!"

Then, with a sudden sweep of his cloak, an expression ineffable, he turned and strode towards the door of an antechamber in the wall beyond. He flung it open and beckoned into the space beyond; then stood back with another deep sardonic bow.

"I told you, M. le petit Chevalier, that I had a surprise. You were unwise—oh, unwise to spurn my gift! It is precious—precious, my dear young friend, beyond all words!"

All the time, as he spoke, I was aware of tired quiet footsteps approaching across the room beyond the door we faced. My heart beat uncontrollably—I moved forward on an instinct. . . .

A shadow filled the frame. Blackadder straightened himself, the evil triumph in his eyes beyond all description in its intensity.

An instant later I was clasped in the poor frail arms of my grandfather! And, as we clung together, the chill quiet whisper of our enemy's voice was in my ear again—and it spoke the phrase that had haunted me since ever I had confronted him in the hold of the *Manon*:

" *La vipère noire*, my friend! Thus triumphs at last. *La vipère noire! . . .*"

PART FOUR

"ARIEL AND ALL HIS QUALITY"

*The narrative resumed from the point of the
meeting at the château de Rohan-Soubise*

by
The Editor

CHAPTER ONE

LA VIPÈRE NOIRE

FOR A LONG moment there was silence in the great library of Rohan-Soubise, broken only by the low moaning of the old Chevalier. He was profoundly moved by his meeting with his grandson—again and again he held him at arm's length as if to assure himself that the boy indeed lived and was well; and then he held him close again in a kind of happy distress.

"Oh, my boy," he said, "—my dear child! After all this time! And I thought you dead—I thought you dead! My heart was nearly broken—I did not wish to live myself. . . ."

Tom, watching, was deeply touched in the spectacle. The old man had aged terribly in the two past years—his hair, which had been grey, was white; his cheeks had fallen in; his eyes were wan and distracted and full of suffering.

Butterfield coughed brusquely—as a man does who is a little ashamed of a sudden wave of feeling.

"Confound you, Blackadder," he said gruffly. "I don't know what it is in the Devil's name you have done——"

"What I have done, Lieutenant?" said the spy sardonically, turning. "What I have *done*, sir? I have surely—for once, as you would say!—done something which is highly commendable by all the standards that you and your like believe in. I have reunited two loving hearts, Lieutenant Butterfield—two loving hearts! And at no small risk, I must ask you to believe. It is one thing to smuggle Moonshine across the Channel—even to smuggle pigeons across the Channel. But human beings, sir—and at a moment when your cursed Admiral Nelson has his eyes upon our every move—that, Lieutenant, is no mean achievement, I assure you. But I did it—and you behold the result—and are more moved than you care to show, I fancy!"

Butterfield indeed had coughed again, and was blinking his eyes rapidly as he gazed at Harry and the old Chevalier. But at Blackadder's sneer he flared up in his old way.

"Deuce take you, sir, for a scoundrelly, ill-bred, weasel-hearted——"

The spy raised his hand, and the old anger flashed in him.

"Enough! I have other things to do than to exchange courtesies with you, Butterfield. Kabal—take this man out. And you, McGuffie—if you can bear to tear yourself away from a scene which obviously enthralls you—take the girl and the seaman there. Leave Cathro here. I want him to stay. . . ."

There was a bustle as Kabal and McGuffie obeyed their Master's orders. The latter indeed had been gaping at the reunion scene with his mouth a round O of wonder. He did not understand the significance of what was happening, but in his sentimental way he had plainly been moved by what he saw—so moved that he stayed entirely dumb, even while he jostled Blue Nose and Mignonne to the door. The last Tom saw of him was his foolishly distressed round face as he closed the door behind Kabal and the others. And then he turned his own attention to Blackadder again. . . .

The spy stood close by the table, fingering a long ornate paper-knife. He watched the two de Rohans with a strange melancholy detachment. And he stayed silent while Harry helped his grandfather forward to a chair. The old man kept a close grip on his grandson —as if terrified at the thought that he might lose him again. Harry, with a quiet sad smile to Tom, crouched down on the floor by the Chevalier's feet. And so they stayed silent, waiting.

The spy was motionless, but for the little movement he made with the knife. With a swift, sharp gesture, he was driving the point of it over and over into the polished top of the table.

Then suddenly he turned—and there came out of him enigmatically, a long deep-drawn sigh. And he spoke —continuing, as it were, the conversation he had begun with Butterfield.

"Yes, I did it," he said, his voice low. "I did it—I brought you across the Channel. But no man knows yet why I did it. . . ."

And then again he was silent; and when he resumed it was to address Tom, who still stood where Kabal had left him, opposite the table. Outside, the shadows were lengthening; darkness gathered in the corners of the old library. Through the window Tom saw the great round nodding shape of the balloon as it filled up with gas. And Blackadder spoke on and on, ignoring at first the two de Rohans in whose home he stood—spoke with a strange detachment, almost, as if half to himself as well as to Tom.

"When I was a boy, Cathro," he said, "—when I was your age, my father died. I remember little of him— I chose to forget. I remember only that I was glad when he died. He was a man unspeakably cruel—not only to me but to my mother—more even to her than to me. She was younger than he was—was a French-woman who met him in Scotland when she was too inexperienced to know mankind and its ways. They married and he brought her to London—and began from that moment the wicked persecution of her for which I could have murdered him, young as I was. He drank heavily. He was morose and despicable—but a clever enough brute in his way—they used to say he dabbled in black magic in the neighbourhood where we lived. But at any rate, whatever he was, whatever he did, I only know that he made her life a misery. When he died—when I was fifteen—it was a relief unutterable to both of us. We left England for France —and from that moment forward I hated England and all it stood for—because of him and the wretched-ness of our life there.

"We were poor—we were desperately poor in France at the first. I worked hard to support us both, but there were still days on end when we had nothing to eat—nowhere to live except wretched hovels of lodgings that we were permitted to occupy out of pity. Is it any wonder that I grew to hate and despise those others who had plenty?—those who lived like this man, in a palace like this one?——"

His voice had been rising as he spoke, and now he turned with a sudden gesture towards the Chevalier de Rohan, who sat motionless, his hand upon Harry's shoulder.

"—who oppressed us and destroyed us, so that they could thrive and flourish in luxury——"

"I oppressed no man," said the Chevalier very quietly. "If you know so much else about us, you must know that. When I lived in this place you have commandeered, in the way I have been brought up to live, I did all I could to alleviate the human suffering I saw all around me."

"Yes! Yes!" hissed the spy, his voice low. "You did!—and it was worse so—it was even worse! Listen, M. le Chevalier—when I was little older than that boy you caress there, I came to you and begged for help. My mother was ill—it was not long after we had come to France. I was desperate and I was penniless. I waited upon you in your house in Paris—I asked for help——"

"If you did, as you say, it would have been given."

"It was! It was! And when you did give it—even while I was buying bread with the money you had lavished on me—I hated you even more than all the others! Because I had had to ask—and because you had given!—because you *could* give! Do you understand that?"

The old Chevalier was silent, his eyes on the tall malignant figure before him.

"I swore that when the day came, you and your family would die as surely as all the others," Blackadder went on. "I swore more than that. I swore that you who had given already would have to give more —and to me, do you understand—to *me*! I knew the great wealth of your family—I knew that somewhere, hidden away in some corner, there was a great hoard of jewels and old gold and silver—the famous Treasure of the de Rohans! And I vowed that it would be *mine* —when the day of reckoning came at last!"

He paused, and for a moment resumed his stabbing at the table-top with the knife. His pale face had grown paler, his deep eyes burned.

"The day of reckoning did come," he said, speaking more quietly, his voice an edgy menace in the increasing gloom. "You know as well as I that the day of reckoning came. The Revolution. And remembering all things I had suffered, I more than any other man worked hard in those glorious years to bring all aristocrats to justice. I traded on my father's name—the name I bore from the man I hated: Blackadder. Oh, a common enough name in Scotland, my friends— a simple name, borne by many worthy people. But in my ears it had a ring and an association that I despised. Nevertheless, I used it—I used it then, in those days, as I used it again two years ago in your beloved Dorset. At the time of the Revolution who was I, M. le

Chevalier? Who was *I*? I was the man whom every aristocrat in France held in terror—the informer who found them wherever they might be hiding—who brought them to the guillotine! I was, M. le Chevalier, that famous Black Adder of the Terror!—*La Vipère Noire!* "

Kneeling on the floor beside his grandfather, Harry looked up at the tall crooked shape of their enemy, looming above them.

"I know," he said shortly. "I realised it. Always, at the back of my mind, there was the echo of that. I was too young to remember, but I had been told—a hundred times. It was *La Vipère Noire* who pursued us when we made our first attempt at escape——"

"It was!—it always was *La Vipère Noire* in those days! But you never thought to connect *La Vipère Noire* with Blackadder—not openly. Nor did you, M. le Chevalier—not even when you lived in Dorset and heard of the dreaded Blackadder—it never crossed your mind that I was the same as that other Black Adder who had found you when you tried to escape the guillotine. Perhaps you chose to forget *La Vipère Noire* when you settled in England—but I never forgot you! It was why, above all other places that Blackadder the smuggler might have flourished in, I chose that one place—because I had traced you there; and when the moment was ripe—when I had served my country as a spy in those times—when that was over I would have turned on you and disclosed myself—and done what else it was I had to do! "

His voice had risen again—echoed round the tall

bare walls. He stayed for a moment perfectly still, then suddenly he stooped forward, and his face was twisted again in fury.

"Wait, wait," he said. "There is more—infinitely more. You tried once to escape from this house to England during the Revolution—when you had secret word that you were to be arrested. You got as far as the coast. I—*La Vipère*—discovered your plan in time, and you were pursued and brought back. You were thrown into prison and condemned to die like the dogs of aristocrats you were. But why were you not executed at once—why were you kept waiting for so long in La Force? Because, my friend, I had a reason for keeping you alive! I remembered my oath: that the famous Treasure of the de Rohans was some day to be mine. I knew that when you attempted to escape you would either have tried to take the treasure with you, or you would have hidden it somewhere in France to be reclaimed later. You did not have it with you—therefore it was still hidden in France. Was it?—Was it?"

He hissed the last words venomously, like the viper his name proclaimed. The old Chevalier looked up at him. He was immensely calm and full of a quiet dignity.

"Yes," he said. "It was. The ancient treasure of our house, that you have plainly heard of, was bequeathed to my care. I would not permit it to fall into such hands as yours. It was too dangerous to take with me —of course I hid it."

"I knew it! And I aimed to find out from you where you had hidden it. I had work to do—other work as *La Vipère Noire*. But as soon as that was accomplished, I meant to come to you in La Force and make you tell me where the treasure was—*make you tell me* do you understand? Yet before I did—before I did——"

He hesitated; and his face was suddenly bitter—with even a hint of strange tragedy upon it.

"You escaped from La Force," he resumed, his tone full of hatred. "You escaped. And in escaping——"

Again he hesitated: it was as if he found difficulty for a moment in speaking. But he did speak at last, his voice low again:

"—all my old hatred for you increased a thousand-fold. Do you know why?—why? Because you forced me then to destroy the one creature in all the world I ever loved! . . .

"She had married again—my mother had married again, two years after our arrival in France. A man named Lazaire, a simple fellow, now dead. Lazaire was a gaoler at La Force. Because of that boy there—" (with a gesture to Harry) "—my mother, his wife, took pity upon you when you were in prison, awaiting the scaffold. She did not know of my plans for you—she knew nothing. Only that you had a child with you in the prison there—and out of the goodness of her heart she gave you permission to walk sometimes in the yard. You know how you betrayed her goodness to you—how you used that mite of freedom to plan a second escape. You succeeded. All four of you might have got away had you not met a crowd of revolutionaries in the streets that day. Two of you were restrained by the crowd—the other two, you and the boy, escaped to England. The two caught up in the crowd were recognised and taken back to prison—and it was I who recognised them—I who also joined the crowd that day! I recognised them too late—not until you and the boy had gone out of my reach. But I recognised *them* at least, and they were guillotined. . . .

"There was an inquiry as to how you had escaped. And it was found—by me, my friends, by *me*!—that it was the wife of Lazaire who had made it possible. The law was irrevocable. The wife of Lazaire had to die, innocent as she had been. She did die. And I watched her die. . . ."

For the last time he paused. He had been speaking abruptly in short sharp sentences. Now he straightened himself, and his voice rose.

"Do you wonder," he cried, "—do you wonder that I swore that the day would come when I would destroy you?—you and all your line? In all the long years of the first war, when I fought and worked for my country, I lost all trace of you—I knew no more than that you were in England. And for that reason too, as well as that older one my father had bequeathed me, I hated England, and worked and lived for Bonaparte. When I went to England myself—as Abershaw—I succeeded in finding you; and chose that corner to work from as Blackadder, the harmless smuggler who was also a spy. That you know. What you did not know was that when Blackadder's work was done, I would confront you as *La Vipère Noire*. And before I destroyed you I would still find out that old secret that has haunted me through all these years. I would find out from you—for myself—at last—where lies the Treasure of the House of de Rohan! "

He strode forward, looming over the two dark figures before him.

"When I found you on the beach, boy—when you surprised my secret—I meant to kill you. It was Kabal who reminded me who you were—in my first blind rage against you I had almost forgotten. I knew that it was unlikely that the secret of the treasure would have been passed to you, young as you were. But I knew also that this old man would still have sufficent pride in him not to disclose the secret easily to me or any other. I saw suddenly, however, that with you in my power I had a hold on him. We came to France. And when the time was ripe I brought him to France too. I had sent a message to him secretly, before, that his grandson was alive. An agent of mine went to him one night and told him that if he followed, he would be taken to where that grandson was. He did follow—naturally he did. I smuggled him across the Channel. I brought him here. I have him here. And at last I have you here too. He knows the secret I long to find. And he will tell me what it is. He will be tortured until he does."

"You can torture me as you will," said the Chevalier —and it seemed to Tom that he had never been more dignified than he was at that moment. "I shall never tell."

"You will tell! I said you would be tortured till you did."

"I do not fear pain, sir."

"I know that—I recognised it from the start. I did not underestimate you. But you will still be tortured till you tell! Not physically. Beyond that. Because, Chevalier, because——"

And he straightened himself to his full monstrous height.

"—because the boy will be tortured before your eyes! —and that you will *not* be able to bear!"

The old aristocrat stayed for a moment utterly stunned. Then he struggled to his feet, his hand outstretched towards the enemy.

"The boy does not know," he said, his voice trembling, "—he does not know——"

"I did not suppose he knew. If I had, I would have tried to find out from him long ago—I have had ample opportunity. But *you* know—and through him you will tell!"

And with a last triumphant gesture, he strode towards the door.

"Kabal," he cried. "Kabal! Come here, Kabal! *It is the time!*"

CHAPTER TWO

THE STRAPPADO

KABAL LEADING, they passed through the room where McGuffie guarded Butterfield, Mignonne and Blue Nose. The Scot had gone pale. As Blackadder strode past him he made a gesture as if to speak to him; but held back, and so lost the opportunity.

They went down a flight of winding stone steps to a great underground chamber of bare stone walls. Tom was sick in the heart—he looked at Harry, pushed forward in the grasp of the Master-spy, the old Chevalier pathetically by his side. And he had a deep sense of guilt: it was his fault, he felt, that Harry was where he was—it had been his idea at the outset of all that they should visit the cove to spy on Blackadder; and from that all their long bitter experience had sprung—the storm, the wreck, the imprisonment, the escape attempt that had failed, and now this. . . .

Blackadder, holding a pistol, gestured the Chevalier to a small wooden chair; and when he had sat on it, Kabal rapidly bound him there, his neck jerked back so that he was forced to face straight ahead. Then he seized Harry roughly and bound his hands before him at the wrists. The boy was pale but his gaze was steadfast, his jaw firmly set.

In the ceiling of the underground chamber was **a**

crude wooden pulley, a stout smooth rope passing over it. One end of the rope ran to a cleat on one of the walls; the other dangled loosely within a few feet of the floor.

Kabal worked fast and with a practised skill. When Harry was tied he led him forward till he stood by the dangling rope. Rapidly he looped it across his chest and beneath his armpits. Then, making a slip-knot behind his shoulders, he led the slack upwards and passed it with a cunning twist through the cord that bound the boy's hands, which were now stretched high above his head. He moved to the cleat and took in the slack over the pulley—and Harry was pulled upright, until he barely touched the floor with his toes. His face contorted for a moment as the rope bit into his chest and shoulders with the strain.

Throughout, Blackadder had stayed silent. Now he signalled to Kabal to hold, and turned slowly towards the Chevalier. The Frenchman, a beading of sweat upon his brow, breathed deeply as he held the rope taut. His face too was drawn and strained—a hint in it of distaste for what he had to do, perhaps. But a determination too to serve the Master he worked for and whose paler shadow he was.

"Chevalier," said Blackadder, his voice its old edgy menace, "I present to you the celebrated Strappado, one of the most ancient, simplest, yet deadliest torments ever invented by ingenious mankind. You observe the principle? At a signal from me Kabal there will raise the boy to the ceiling by means of the pulley. At a further signal he will release a length of the rope—

and the boy will fall. But not to the ground—to within a few centimetres of the ground. In the weight of his fall, in the sudden jerk at the end of it, every bone in his body will be racked in an unbelievable excruciation. The rope is so threaded that it too will contract in the movement—his arms, his chest, his shoulders—all will take the strain. The first time it is bearable; but when he rises again, and when he falls again—and again—I can assure you, M. le Chevalier, that it is worse than the rack! That is its beauty—that and its simplicity. Thus the Strappado! "

He signalled to Kabal, who pulled upon the rope until Harry's feet were some four inches from the ground. His face convulsed for a moment as the rope round his chest and through his wrists bit further into his flesh.

"I give you one chance, Chevalier," went on Blackadder. "One chance. That you will die is certain—I have sworn it. But at least I promise you that the boy will not be tortured. Death for both of you will be made easy, *if*—and only if—you tell me where the Treasure lies. Where did you hide it when you fled fifteen years ago? Speak now, and the boy will be cut down. Refuse to speak, and I signal to Kabal to proceed."

The Chevalier, unable to move, to make any gesture, mouthed for a moment silently. His lips were crusted with a little fleck of foam, his eyes were tormented beyond measure. He might have spoken—he might have disclosed the secret; but Harry, in a low firm tone, broke silence before him.

"No, Grandfather. Never tell him—never! I can bear it."

The spy laughed shortly and evilly.

"We shall see, M. le petit Chevalier! We shall see. . . . Kabal—do your worst, man!"

In an instant the rope was pulled tight—and Harry swung high in the air until his head almost touched the pulley. He had closed his eyes, and Tom saw that he bit his lips until a little trickle of blood showed. He stayed poised so for a long moment.

"No—no!" cried the Chevalier. "I will tell—I will!"

The spy's eyes flamed.

"Release, Kabal!" he cried, almost screaming in the sudden ferocity of his feeling. "Once for good fortune! Release!"

The rope screeched over the pulley and Harry fell. Tom closed his eyes. And when he opened them a moment later it was to see Harry dangling a bare two inches from the ground. His face was drained of all blood in the sudden agony—its icy whiteness relieved only by the little red trickle at his chin from his lips. But he had not cried out.

The Chevalier spoke only in a whisper—he was utterly broken.

"His chest," he said, his voice only a whisper. "The mark on the boy's breast. That is the secret—the lines behind the ancient crest. The crest in the hallway above—seek behind it according to the lines and the instructions on the design. That is where the Treasure lies. That is the chart I made. . . ."

With a cry Blackadder sprang forward. He ripped

viciously at Harry's shirt—and there, wealed across by the bite of the rope, Tom saw the tattoo mark he had gazed on so long before on the beach at Lytchett: the ancient crest of the de Rohans, behind it the enigmatic network of lines in a seemingly incomprehensible maze. . . .

"At last, at last!" cried the Master-spy. And he ripped at the rope itself so as to see the sign more clearly.

But at the moment there was a cry from above them, and the sound of a shot; and with a scream Kabal, clutching a shattered wrist, released the rope at the cleat so that Harry sagged forward and his feet met the ground.

With an oath Blackadder swung round, his pistol ready. And it was McGuffie's voice—almost melancholy in its strange quietness—that spoke:

"Drop it, Maister—oh, Maister, ye'll hae to drop your wee gun, man! I've got ye covered at the hert, sir!"

The Scotsman stood at the top of the stone stairway. Beside him were Butterfield and the others—Butterfield with a small still-smoking pistol in his own hand which lingered in the direction of the moaning Kabal.

"McGuffie," cried the spy. "By all that's devil-ish——"

"Aye, sir—by all that's devilish! Oh, ye should never have done it, Maister! I've followed ye and I've listened to ye and I've served ye like the saft weak cratur I am. But ye should never have set to torturing the laddie—na, na, no' that! I cannae thole a torturin'—and never bairns, never bairns. Ye went too far at that, sir!"

Blackadder was as a man struck in a paralysis. His pistol arm had dropped by his side and now he released the weapon itself, which clattered on the floor. Mignonne and Blue Nose had hurried down the stairway from behind the others, and now she was tearing frenziedly at Harry's bonds while the old seaman set to releasing the Chevalier.

"McGuffie," mouthed the spy at last, "—I command you——"

"Na, na, sir—save your breath. I've never liked this ploy we were on—no' since ever ye brought the poor auld soul there frae England and I had a kind o' inkling what was in your mind. It was Kabal tellt me what ye aimed to do when ye were speirin' at these twa in the library. I thocht then I'd hae to finish wi' ye, Maister —and when I heard the auld man gi'e a yell, and kent ye'd begun your torturin', I had to gi'e in to my conscience—even if it was to be against his Nainsel, and me just a poor lost sinner. I let this lot free and gi'ed the Lieutenant a wee gun. Hech, hech, I'm sorry, Maister—I'm real sorry too, but ye see——"

And even at that moment it seemed as if he might embark upon one of his interminable speeches. But by now, Tom assisting her, Mignonne had reached the top of the steps again with Harry, Blue Nose also following behind with the Chevalier. With a sudden howl of unutterable rage, Blackadder acted. He stooped and seized his pistol again; but before he could raise and aim it, there was a little crack and puff from the weapon in McGuffie's hand.

"Oh, Maister, Maister!" he said, in a tone of strange sorrow.

The spy staggered back, clutching his shoulder. And on the instant the others were through the door at the top of the stairway. Butterfield slammed it behind them, fumbling for a moment with the key at the rusty lock.

Somehow, struggling with the almost insensible Chevalier and the dazed Harry, they made for the main doorway, McGuffie following. They reached the high winding stairway leading to the open grounds and staggered somehow down it; then made for cover among the bushes. By now it was almost dark—a few lights glimmered in the huts and tents beyond them. But they were as yet unobserved—there were no soldiers or sentries near the château.

At any moment behind them they expected the sounds of pursuit—the rusty lock of the cellar door could never be expected to hold Blackadder and Kabal for more than a moment. They stumbled forward, breathless and distressed, with no notion where they might be heading.

Suddenly, above them, loomed a monstrous dark shape—an instant of nightmare in that moment of moments: a round blank idiot face, blind and nodding. And a single sentry, a man stunned and useless in the astonishment of their appearance, confronted them.

"Deuce take you for a dead man!" barked Butterfield; and drove his fist full in the man's gaping face. The fellow crumpled with a small strange sigh.

The great basket of the balloon swayed and creaked

before them. There was no need for words—they knew, all of them, on the instant, that the one chance of escape in thousands was before them. Somehow they clambered over the edge of the car—and as they did so there was a cry and a rising commotion from the direction of the château. Over the bushes they saw the figure of Blackadder running at the pace of a madman towards them. Behind him was Kabal, behind him again a straggled group of soldiers, some firing even as they ran.

"The mooring ropes," cried Butterfield. "Cut them—cut them! Confound it, we have no knife——"

"I've aye got that auld whinger of mine," said McGuffie calmly. And he drew the long half-sword with which he had threatened the boys in the cottage at Lytchett.

"Are we safe? Are we a' in?"

He slashed with the great knife's razor edge at the straining mooring ropes at each corner of the basket. The balloon lurched helplessly for a moment—then reared itself; and at last, as Butterfield threw out a bag of sand that lay in the floor of the car, it soared wildly high in the air. And far below them, before he was swallowed in darkness, Tom saw the suddenly dwarf-like figure of the spy, his arms upraised, his twisted face a mere small patch of white against the sweeping sable of his cloak. It was as if, for an instant, he were a great bird, crouching ready to leap after them. But already they were high in the air beyond him; and a moment later the very sound of the rifle shots of the soldiers died away and all was a strange velvet silence.

CHAPTER THREE

THE BALLOON

(Being a paper contributed by George Whitelaw
Butterfield, R.N., b. 1775, d. 1809)

Editor's Note: *When I found the Cathro-Rowan papers
relating to the whole adventure, this brief essay, stained and
faded from age, was among them. Attached to it was a note
in Cathro's handwriting which ran: "It was our design for
many years to build a full account of our activities in the two
years 1803-1805. For various reasons Mr. Rowan and I
have been unable to begin work on our own contributions to
this account until towards the end of our lives. In the year
1809, however, shortly before his gallant death in the ill-
fated Expedition to Walcheren, our friend, George Butterfield, wrote out a description of one of the episodes in the
adventure which he was peculiarly qualified to deal with:
namely, our flight from the Château of Rohan-Soubise in a
balloon. He was to have written more, although as he
claimed he had no pretensions as a literary man; but his
brave death intervened. This paper, however, I have kept
through all the years, and will add it in the proper place in
my own account."*

*Thus wrote Admiral Cathro, at the time when he began his
own compilation (which, of course, in its own turn was never
fully completed). The Butterfield paper fits so exactly into*

195   G.

place at this point of the tale that I insert it in its entirety and exactly as written, the Lieutenant's style and even his occasionally peculiar spelling, being quite untouched by my or any other hand.—S. McF.

My NAME is George Whitelaw Butterfield. I am honoured in being an officer of His Majesty's Navy. God Save the King!

In the year 1805 I escaped from a chatto in France by means of an observation balloon cut loose from its moorings. I had the following for companions: Thomas Cathro; Harry de Rohan; the Chevalier de Rohan; Elijah Quince, A.B., of H. M. Navy also; and last but not least Mlle. Mignonne de Barbaroux, of St. Pol-de-Leon. Also one Habbakuk McGuffie, a renegade, but his defection mittigated in his having assisted us to make the escape.

I held myself from the moment of our embarkation to be Officer in Charge.

Apart from my Rank, it so befell that I had had some previous experience of ballooning.

In the year 1800, on shore leave from the Fleet, I went aloft on several occasions with a friend at Vauxhall; at which resort, of course, ballooning had for some time been fashionable sport.

I understood, therefore, some of the navigation principles of the balloon.

At the start of our flight I threw out much ballast, so to rise quickly. The car was heavily loaded, with as many as seven persons aboard. Below us our enemies were soon swept out of sight as I threw out still more ballast and we continued to rise.

It was by this time fully dark. As our eyes grew accustomed to this, we saw many lights glimmering below us, from hovels and such of the French. Far away was a great cluster of twinkling, which we took to be Paris; and knowing Paris was south of the chatto, we took our direction thus.

A gentle wind blew; its direction SE; we, therefore, to our inexpressible joy, were making in the way we wished to go: *viz*, the coast; and proceeded at a speed of some 2 knots, as far as I could reckon.

We stopped rising after about 10 minutes. At this point (what height I know not) the rarer air equalled in volume our own weight; and so we hung steady. For some time the gas had been blowing off into the car through the neck, which hung uncommonly low in that craft. This process is normal, of course, in order to keep the gas in the envelop the same pressure as that of the outside air; but because of the very low neck it occasioned us much discomfort. In particular it distressed, with its evil smell, the Chevalier, who was weak in the experience he had passed through; and the boy de Rohan, fresh from a bout of torment under the fiendish Strapado.

Quince, the girl and the Scot McGuffie attended our sick. McGuffie seemed in a strange relief. He sang jolly songs now, in his uncouth dialect. He seemed happy from his release from Blackadder the Spy; it was as if he had for some time secretly been serving him against his will. As indeed he said was the case.

The other boy, Cathro, kept watch with me.
So we stayed until dawn.

In the morning it was bitter cold, for it was winter starting now. Our sick were much distressed. I pulled the valve cord to lessen height somewhat; but was chary of coming too low for two reasons, *viz*:

1. I wished to conserve gas, lest

2. We were being pursued. For if we came too low we might fall within gunshot length. Knowing the direction of the wind, it was more than like that Blackadder would attempt pursuit. He knew now his only hope to get the Tresure was in studying the map engraved upon H. de R's chest, which gave its whereabouts, working from the point of the main crest in the chatto by means of the maze of direction lines and the distances marked thereon. The Chevalier explained to us (by now somewhat recovered) that on his first arrival in England he had had the tattoo made upon the boy, so that there would forever be a secret record of where the Tresure lay. He intended before he died to tell the boy the working of this cipher upon his own chest, so that when all was done, and entrance to France was freely possible, the Tresure c'd be reclamed by its rightful owner, *viz*, the boy.

In mid-morning we saw far below us a river winding; and took it for the Seine. We saw the little boats on it, and the people in them looking up.

I lowered further. The wind was freshening and we proceeded more rapidly; but still merely drifted. I wished indeed that the great problem of dirigible flight had been solved, so that we could steer—the one drawback in Balloon flight. (Memo: might something be done with sweeps, or a kind of broad light oar?—as it were the air as the sea, the balloon propeled as is a boat?)

Suddenly we saw at one point, beyond the left bank of the river, that we were pursued indeed. A knot of men went forward with us, following us across fields and c. And it was as we c'd see, even at that height, the Enemy, and his French fellow Lewis Kabbal; and some other fellows also, military.

"Ay, 'tis the Maister," thereupon said McGuffie in his patois. "He will never give up, his Nainsel won't. Not now. And pity upon us all if he should catch us now."

The group below halted at this point; and there was a firing of rifles in the air to us; and the balls passed very near. One pierced the envelop, but its strength was spent; moreover, the treated silk of the envelop sealed over, and our craft's wound was not serious. But if they peppered her sufficiently we might suffer. So I threw over more ballast (the last) and rose up; and had the satisfaction to see the sandbag of ballast fall near Blackadder below, and his horse reared up and near threw him.

The wind freshened and we made pace; to such extent that we left the pursuer behind here. We had lost some gas in the two descents and could not make very much height—sufficient, but not a prodigious deal. The lower part of the envelop was flabby, and flapped to and fro above our heads.

So night fell again. We were weak and much disturbed in want of food. McGuffie had upon him some bread and a flask of the liquor of his country, uskebaw;* this last we gave to the sick and shared the bread.

This second night it rained much, which weighted the envelop and lowered us; but we also caught some moisture in the flabby lower part of the envelop and so quenched thirst.

In the dawn we scanned below most anxiously for pursuers; but there were none, praise be to heaven. We drifted now very slowly in the weight of the sodden envelop, and I had no more ballast to throw.

When dawn broke we saw we were over sea; and reckoned, from our memories of the contours, that we were somewhere crossing the north Normandy coast. The morning was misty and wet, but we saw at one point a cluster of houses near the shore; a fishing town or village, which perhaps was Isigny, or even Formignes, where we had been before when we were retaken. But still no sign of pursuit.

By this time the envelop flapped badly, for not only was it heavy from wet, but there must have been a leak of gas. I cast desperately about in the car for something to throw over to raise us; for if we started a "down-run," as it is called, we could crash badly. I threw over the grappling iron, cut loose; and divested myself of my outer clothes; and McGuffie and Cathro likewise. We gained a little height; and now drifted over land once more.

Below us, during this day, were many people much

* Whisky! Butterfield was trying to reproduce the sound of the old Scottish word for the spirit, usquebaugh, which McGuffie would have used.—Ed.

surpriz'd and looking up and waving. Once or twice some camps of military; but they took us for observation officers training, and but flagged us, and called up, hallooing; and we heard their voices very far-off and faint, but clear, rising up to us in the airy expanses of the heaven.

Once only, late afternoon, did we see what might have been pursuit; a little knot, as before, far back, on a narrow road, moving our way. But very faint in the thickening weather; and we were not sure. Perhaps harmless travellers.

Towards evening, the coast again, ahead; and height still losing—and no hope now of further ballast. I had no other course but to land—and to land before we struck over the sea, for now it would be open ocean.

I now blamed myself strongly for throwing over the grappling iron before, for it would have been much help. I could do nothing else but loose the valve, so as to lose gas; and pray for a good landing.

I lowered and further lowered. I told my companions to hold tightly. I stayed at the valve-rope to release more gas. The envelop above was half-deflated; and so began to act as a parachute in the wind, and to "drag." We were very low. Suddenly Cathro shouted there were some fishing boats, ashore, a little away. I saw the use they might be to us if we were indeed pursued, so pulled heavily upon the valve cord.

We bumped; and were thrown in a heap inside the car. We rose again. But the great envelop dragged badly. I pulled the valve cord with all my strength. The envelop sagged and fell down in a heap before us

—in the sea. The basket heeled over and we decanted on wet sand; and it dragged forward away from us; and left us stranded. And the car dragged over some sharp small rocks and was ripped before it came to rest when the great envelop settled in the water. It was Providence we decanted when we did.

Thus our flight ended; we lying on the wet sand. And perhaps, for all we knew, pursuit close behind us; for all along our enemy must have known our drift from the wind; and, as we had seen, at one point was close. Here ends my account. May heaven be praised for our deliverance!

(*And so I resume my own version of what befell at this stage of the adventure.—Editor*).

CHAPTER FOUR

GLORY

IN A RECKONING they made long afterwards, Tom Cathro and his companions were on a bleak and deserted stretch of shore on the west coast of Normandy, near Carteret perhaps. From where they lay on the sand, the little cluster of fishing boats mentioned by Butterfield were a quarter of a mile away.

They were famished from want of food, cold from the long exposure. But at least in the interval both Harry and the Chevalier had recovered some strength, and so, in a little procession, they made their way forward in the gathering dusk.

As they neared the boats they saw that there were perhaps half-a-dozen of them. They were in an ill state of repair—only two, as far as they could judge, were sea-worthy. Tattered sails were raised in these, as if in readiness for going out. A small breeze blew off-shore.

Above the boats, on a prominence, were two tumble-down cottages. They went towards them, Butterfield and McGuffie going ahead. A curious friendship had grown up between these two during the flight in the balloon, patriot though one of them was, renegade the other. They were the only two of the party armed: Butterfield with the pistol which McGuffie had given him, now reloaded; and McGuffie himself with his own pistol and his famous "whinger."

A squat, dirty-looking man stared foolishly at them from one of the cottages as they approached. Behind him in the gloom was a slatternly woman, surrounded by a great silent brood of pinched, wide-eyed children.

They made known their wishes, the two leaders holding their weapons prominently before them: some refreshment, a brief rest, and then—with a gesture to the shore—one at least of the seaworthy boats. They were poor enough vessels indeed for a voyage designed to end in England, but the risk had to be taken—and there was little time to waste. Perhaps indeed, at that moment, Blackadder was close upon them.

The fisherman, with an ill-grace, stood aside for them to enter, and the woman set before them a bowl of "crowdie," as McGuffie called it (a thick clotted cheese), and some stale black bread. A flagon of a coarse red wine from the fisherman himself completed the repast.

They ate ravenously, while the forlorn children of the fisherfolk gauped foolishly at them. And it was while they sat back, refreshed to a degree, poor though the food had been, that they heard, echoing weirdly across the bleak flats, the low call of an owl, twice-repeated.

McGuffie was on his feet in an instant, his round face suddenly tense.

"It's him!" he said in a low voice a-tremble. "His Nainsel! He's traced us, deil that he is! We maun get down—we maun get down and away! . . ."

In Tom too the call of the owl had raised an apprehension, remembering it as he did from the night of terror on the Lytchett beach long before. He moved forward with Mignonne to help the old Chevalier, his heart pounding. Were they to be retaken yet again? when they had gone so far? And this time. . . . He shuddered, with a glance at Harry.

Rapidly they made for the shore—for the two sea-worthy boats. And it was as they reached them that they heard the owl-call repeated, closer at hand; and a shot rang out—and old Blue Nose stumbled and fell forward on the sand. He rose on the instant, but unsteadily, and clasped his upper left arm with his hand.

Another shot from higher up on the beach went wide; and by this time the enemy was in sight, out-lined against the gloomy sky. Blackadder and Kabal —alone; advancing implacably down the beach to-wards them, two tall and menacing figures. . . .

Unhurriedly, but with an air of authority, Butter-field directed the Chevalier into one of the boats. He made Mignonne follow him and then Blue Nose, instructing the latter to trim sail and make ready to push off. The old seaman's wound was skin-deep only, and he had bound it rapidly and with his kerchief, pull-ing the knot tight with his teeth. But he had gone pale a little in the pain of it.

"Now, boy, into the boat with them," said Butter-field to Harry. "We three shall follow in the other, so as to leave none for these devils to follow us in—the rest there are staved and rotten. Quickly!"

For an instant Harry hesitated by the water's edge, glancing at Tom, as if wishing to stay with him. Then he turned towards the Chevalier. The old man sat with Mignonne, his eyes wide and staring, as if the long and bitter experience had proved all too much for him in the end. He no longer fully knew where he was or what was happening. And, at the spectacle, the boy moved forward into the water and set his hands on the stern, to push off and then leap aboard. Blue Nose, at the tiller, had trimmed the sail and stayed calmly waiting further orders.

But at the moment there was a cry from the enemy further up the beach. Harry half-turned, and saw that Blackadder and Kabal had stopped. One of the spy's pistols was empty—hung down by his side. The other pointed towards the group at the waterline.

"Wait!" he cried, his voice echoing over the bleak deserted flats. "Butterfield—there is one chance more! Give me the boy—give me the boy and the Scotsman, Butterfield, and you shall go free!"

"No, sir!" said the little Lieutenant brusquely. "I will give you neither. I have suffered enough at your hands. You are a thing of evil and an enemy of my country. I will give you nothing but lead before I go, sir!"

He raised his own pistol sharply and fired. The spy did not move. But as Tom watched he saw an angry red sear across his white cheek. And, still implacable, he swung his second pistol towards Harry, still poised at the stern of the first boat.

"Lord help us," breathed McGuffie. "He's mad—

he's mad, sir! We must in the boat and away, Lieutenant. . . ."

"The boy!" came the spy's thin voice—and there was madness in it indeed. "I must have the boy!—alive or dead I shall have the boy! I need him, for what he wears upon his breast!"

And as he spoke he fired—and Harry, with a cry, spun round and fell. As he did so he pushed against the stern of the smack and it thrust forward and so was launched. Tom himself leapt forward into the water and raised up his friend. An ugly stain had spread across Harry's temple, but even at the first glance he saw that the wound was slight and Harry was conscious.

"He's all right," he called to Butterfield. "Flesh wound!" And he stumbled across to the gunwale of the second boat, dragging the stunned Harry with him.

"Go on, go on, Quince!" cried the little Lieutenant to Blue Nose. "Take them out—home—to England! We shall follow—we shall pick you up off-shore. Go on—go on, man!"

The old seaman turned. The mottled brown sails of the little boat filled up. For a moment the slim figure of Mignonne could be seen, standing up in the bow; and a cry from her came back across the rapidly widening space between the smack and the shore. But she had heard Tom's shout to Butterfield and knew that Harry was safe. The little boat went forward rapidly, into the gloom falling over the sea, and was in an instant a mere dim shadow receding.

And all the time, Blackadder was striding implacably forward again, Kabal behind him. McGuffie had clambered into the second boat, and now helped Tom across the gunwale with Harry. On the skyline above the beach there was a clustering of dim figures as the rest of Blackadder's pursuit party assembled to come forward. The little Lieutenant saw the boys aboard and set his hand upon the stern to push off to follow the other boat in the darkness, to safety at last. And at the moment there was a cry, monstrous again in the silence, from the spy behind them; and with a great last leap he covered the intervening space and hurled himself on Butterfield. He had fired his own last shot—he threw his pistol wildly before him; and as it flew across the little boat it caught McGuffie a glancing blow on the side of the face and sent him spinning.

Butterfield was half-in-half-out of the boat when the spy attacked him. He was ill-balanced to defend himself. Blackadder fought in a maniac fury of thrashing arms and legs, his great cloak sweeping all about them, his white flaming face a mask of unutterable rage. But it was the very violence of his attack that frustrated him—that and Butterfield's lack of balance. The two figures toppled together into the cramped stern of the smack; and the impetus of the spy's great leap pushed the little vessel forward from the sand and out upon the water.

From high up on the beach there were shouts from the pursuing *gens d'armes* and some ragged shots which went wide in the gloom. Tom struggled from his position forward to the tiller. The sails had already filled, the boom swung out above his head as he crouched below the gunwale.

In the well beneath him Butterfield and Blackadder still struggled together—as they had done long before in the longboat during the great storm. He reached the tiller and grasped it—and found himself face to face across the stern gunwale with Kabal. The Frenchman had waded forward, still with the same dogged silence in which he had crossed the beach. The water reached to his chest, but still he had advanced until, at the moment of Tom's arrival in the stern, he had been able to set his hands upon the gunwale, and strained with every sinew in his huge body to hold the boat from further movement.

But McGuffie, recovered from the blow from the pistol, was on his own feet again by this time. He saw the danger at a glance and raised his own pistol. He fired; and Tom, his face close to the Frenchman's, saw a small round hole appear suddenly in his temple. Kabal's mouth opened—he gave a sudden small moan of surprise rather than pain. He raised one hand to his brow and touched the wound with a curious remote gentleness. The other hand still gripped the smack's gunwale; but even as Tom regarded him in a grave horror, he saw it twist and release. The boat went forward; and before the darkness swallowed him away, Tom saw Kabal still standing, his head and shoulders high above the sea, one hand at his brow, the other outstretched, the fingers convulsing as if still aiming to grasp at his enemies, even in the moment of death. And then he was gone. . . .

And simultaneously, behind him, Tom heard a great shuddering sigh from Butterfield. He looked round— and saw the little Lieutenant stagger backwards and fall crumpling in a momentary exhaustion on one of the seats. Below, in the well, was the huddled motionless shape of the spy stunned to unconsciousness from Butterfield's last great blow above his heart. . . .

And so, at the end, the adventure moved towards its climax. It was late September in that year of 1805 when the little fishing boat moved out from the shore of Normandy. It was a wet cold night, with only a little wind, and they were uncertain of direction. Always as they went they kept a lookout for the other smack but in the darkness there was no sign. They cast to and fro for long hours, calling across the water; but the delay on the beach had given Blue Nose too much of a start and he must have taken a different direction. For all they knew, they themselves might still be being pursued—the *gens d'armes* on shore had perhaps found other boats and embarked to follow them; and so in the end they gave up the search and moved forward, away from the land. They prayed only that Blue Nose, despite his wound, would be able, out of his long experience of seamanship, to take the little boat to England in safety.*

Harry's wound was slight—in the gloom on the beach Blackadder's aim had been bad. McGuffie

---

* As indeed he did. The voyage lasted some three days, it seems, and towards the end of it the old Chevalier was almost a dead man. Mignonne too suffered greatly from exposure. But Blue Nose, a remarkable sailor of the old school, steered the vessel somehow towards the English Channel where they were picked up at last by a fishing fleet of our own off the Isle of Wight.—Ed.

dressed it carefully—he had a skill in such tendernesses. The boy was weakened from the torture, the long exposure in the balloon, and finally the wound itself. But there was nothing fundamentally wrong with him—nothing that rest in due time would not cure.

As for Blackadder, towards dawn he recovered consciousness. When he did, however, it was to find himself bound, unable to move from his crouched position in the well. And so he stayed, his face a pale mask, expressionless; his eyes closed; only his long thin hands in a constant nervous twitching motion.

They were far from the coast. All round them stretched a grey calm sea, merging with the wet grey of the sky. There were no signs of further pursuit. In silence, worn out, famished again with hunger, they drove on, heading northwards as they believed, but with no real sense of where they might indeed be heading.

All day they voyaged. Their eyes were strained as they peered eternally across the grey wastes before them, their lips parched and dry despite the mist of rain which constantly drenched them. They huddled together for warmth, only one of them remaining always at the tiller to steer and to watch the still form of Blackadder. If it had not been for the incessant movement of his hands, the spy might indeed have been dead as he lay there—and even then there came over Tom at times, as he watched the twitching, fascinated —even then it seemed that perhaps the movement was only a reflex after all; perhaps the spy was dead indeed.

and his fingers convulsed as the legs of a frog will convulse when all life has gone out of the body. . . .

But Blackadder at last did open his eyes. He opened them at the great cry which came from Butterfield in the bows in the late afternoon. The little Lieutenant was on his feet and pointing—and his face was lit with a bright crazy triumph.

Tom followed his gesture; and saw, afar off, but still plainly visible in a clearing of the low sea-mist, a little group of noble ships. Their vast hulks, yellow and black, surged in the swell, their sails billowed out in the breeze, their flags were a glory against the sky.

"Now God be praised," said Butterfield, his voice low, its tone full of a profound emotion. "The fleet—our fleet! God save His Noble Majesty! . . ."

His voice broke and he lowered his head. And Tom too rose to his feet—and felt his own heart ready to burst in the great ecstasy of the moment. His eyes, dim with tears, were upon one ship—one huge majestic ship before the others. He knew the flag upon its mainmast—had seen it once at Portsmouth long before —a century before, as it seemed. He raised his arm high in a salute. . . .

It was September 1805; and Vice-Admiral Viscount Nelson, in his flag-ship *Victory* was heading south to Cape Trafalgar.

PART FIVE

"PRIDE, POMP AND CIRCUMSTANCE..."

*The adventure continued and taken
towards its conclusion*

by

Admiral Sir Thomas Cathro

THEY SAY that though a man be fluent in pen, perhaps, and can make a reasonable account of most things that may befall, when it comes to write of an experience that has affected him particularly deeply, then he is troubled and dumb and sits staring from his window chewing his quill, and no words flow.

I may be no full-fledged author, but I have had in my days some little experience of the Gentle Art. As I look from my desk it is to see on the shelf across from me, here in the little house in Lytchett to which I have retired in my age, the compact row of my books—those tomes I have inscribed from time to time in the intervals of my long life's work upon the sea or since I have retired therefrom.* My pen, in short, is fluent *enough*—for most ordinary purposes. But now I am to write of that one great central experience of my life, and so may vouch for the truth of the old saying I mention. I sit and mope and ponder, the vacant white sheet before me; and pour a little wine, perhaps, in the hope to find the inspiration to start; or stroll to the window and look out—and see, this bright summer day, the boys go down to the sea to bathe—as Harry and I went down those long, long years ago. . . .

* The titles of some of them are mentioned in Mr. Rowan's contribution—at the start of Part III.—Ed.

Well, well, it was how it began, after all: with our swim in the cove that old May day—and our stroll thereafter across the dunes with poor Philadelphia (and she long dead, heaven rest her—and in foreign parts, to which she went to marry in '14, I think—or was it '15?). It was how it began; and so I sit to end it somehow, imperfect though the writing down may be. So much has been written already of that glorious day of October half a century past—how may I hope to add to the thousands of expert words? Yet we were involved—Harry and I, and the good Butterfield too—in our own private affairs, even at the height of the great battle; and so I tie those threads at least, even if I leave much else unsaid. . . .

Nelson

He was, it seemed to us when we saw him for the first time, a very little man after all.

We had tacked towards the *Victory* herself in our smack that day; and she bearing down upon us, we drew together in less than the half-hour. The wind was ill; and so we came slowly into her great side, and were secured against the foot of her ladder by some seamen who had descended, and who grappled forth to hold us with their red round faces cheerful and laughing. We held so for long enough to go aboard, Harry assisted in his weakness, Blackadder, bound at the wrists and with his legs held too with a short length of rope, carried to the bows by McGuffie and one of the sailors. And then the smack was cast loose and went drifting, and the last we saw of her she was dipping and flapping her brown sails helplessly in the surge of our wake. So we mounted; and so we confronted him.

He stood regarding us quietly as we went forward, a little smile about his lips. He was straddle-legged upon the quarter-deck, a small group of officers a pace or two away—and one of them, a large tall man with a telescope, I knew to be Captain Hardy, whom once I had seen. He (the Captain) looked quizzically back and forth from us to his Admiral and beloved friend; and no doubt was comparing the neat spruceness of the one with the draggled half-clad weariness of ourselves. Only Blackadder and Harry among us were fully clothed; Butterfield and McGuffie and I had thrown our outer garments over the edge of the balloon-car for ballast.

All about us as we advanced were the sounds of the great ship in motion: the creak and strain of the lines, the tossed wild screaming of the gulls about the stern, the occasional cry of an order from forrard. On the main-deck below us some sailors, their heads bound round with yellow cloths, paused momentarily from their gun-drill to cast curious glances upon us; and then in an instant resumed their labours as one of the officers on the quarter-deck glanced sternly down and signalled.

We remained silent—and I only know that my heart beat strangely as I gazed upon this man whom all England loved. I felt the little muscles of my throat contract and tremble. He, for his part, was still and composed. The loose right arm of his coat, pinned over his chest, flapped loosely a little in the breeze.

His fine-drawn features were pale, blanched as the spotless linen he wore at his collar. Under the green shade that folded out from beneath his hat-brim his eyes shone intense and penetrating, with only the smallest sign of weakness in the right to recall the glory of Calvi eleven years before.

"Well, gentlemen," he said, his voice quiet, a little nasal twang about it, but coming to us clearly, "—well, gentlemen! You come to us out of the sea when we need men most. You are a good omen. Except the tall fellow who scowls—faith, I could almost have thought him Boney himself when I saw you through the glass!—come to surrender or to offer single combat!"

There was a little murmur of laughter from the group of officers. Indeed, as I had often remarked myself, there was something very similar to Napoleon in Blackadder's whole malignant cast—the Napoleon of the early drawings, not the later, when he was fat and puffy; the thin, fanatical Napoleon of the hooked nose and sallow cheeks and baleful eyes.

Butterfield, now that the Admiral had spoken, stepped forward a pace and saluted.

"Second Lieutenant George Butterfield, late of the frigate *Hawk*, my Lord. And at your service to command."

"Butterfield?" said Nelson. "Relative to Eliab Butterfield of the old *Goliath*? Died at Copenhagen—a brave man, sir."

"My father, my lord."

"I knew him well. I welcome you twice as the son

of so fine a man, Lieutenant. As for your own ship—the *Hawk*—she went down in a gale off Plymouth a year since, if I recall."

"I had not known, my lord," said Butterfield. "I have been a prisoner of the enemy for two years with my companions here. We have this moment escaped—after several previous unsuccessful attempts."

"So?" He cast his quizzical glance over us. "You bear all the marks about you indeed. Yet these two are but boys, surely?—how came it they were held prisoner in France?"

"Thomas Cathro, my lord, of Dorset," said Butterfield, gesturing me to stand forward, which I did. "And Harry de Rohan, likewise of Dorset."

"De Rohan? But a French name, Lieutenant. Is the boy French?"

"In name only, your honour," said Harry. "And even that I will change to Rowan when we get back to England."

For an instant an ineffable expression passed over the great Admiral's fine thin face—a look, momentary and fleeting, of sorrow; a little smile of pain.

"When we get back to England, boy? Do you think we *will* get back to England?"

"I believe so, your honour—under your guidance."

"And God's, boy—and God's," murmured Nelson. "Well, well—it will be as Providence directs. . . . Tell me shortly how you did escape, Lieutenant—and how it came that you were ever held."

"We escaped by balloon, my lord—and we were held through the subversive offices of this man who is our prisoner, and who is one of the spies of Bonaparte and a thing of evil. . . ."

And briefly, in a few modest words, Butterfield sketched our story, the while the Admiral stayed listening in his original straddle-legged attitude, his head a little to one side and all the time scanning us closely with his keen eyes, the blind one seeming as live as the other. When Butterfield had finished he turned his gaze upon Blackadder himself, who stood erect and motionless as always, his face an expressionless mask, his huge black cloak flapping round him in the breeze, which had freshened a little since our arrival on deck.

"Blackadder," said Nelson, softly. "I have heard of Blackadder—*La Vipère Noire*. . . . Come forward, Blackadder—forward to face me."

The spy made no move. At the insolence, Captain Hardy made to stride forth himself, as if to force the enemy to obey. But Nelson restrained him with a gesture. He fixed his gaze upon the spy's alabaster face; and he repeated, in a quieter voice still, but a voice that had in it a suggestion of an unutterable power of will:

"Blackadder—come forward, I say! I command you to come forward, sir! "

There was no menace in the tone, no anger; but the man who had uttered the words was a man of men, a force in the world which could not be denied. One instant longer Blackadder hesitated—and then stepped forward.

So they confronted—the spy baleful and defiant, the

great leader calm and full of dignity. From him, as he stood there, his head upraised to gaze in the other's eyes, there came an atmosphere indescribable—the whole essence of his greatness.

"You are an enemy of my King, Blackadder," he said. "You are everything that I hold most despicable—a creature who fights not openly but by subtle contrivance in the dark. I honour a noble foe, but not such as you. You have tormented children and old men—you have played the coward's part always. Worst of all things, you have not fought for your Emperor, which I still could honour a man for doing, even though I regard your Emperor as a power of evil in the land; you have fought for your own selfish ends—and those ends most vicious of all: cruel revenge and sordid personal gain. . . . When all is over, Blackadder, you will be taken and dealt with as you deserve—but not before fair trial, for I will not descend to such methods as you yourself would use and have used. Yet it will go hard if after that fair trial you are not shot dead. . . ."

He paused. Throughout, his gaze had been intent upon the master-spy. Blackadder, for his part, had stared as hardly at Nelson—the old hypnotic stare, which he had used so often upon us. But now it was he who lowered his eyes—and for a moment the pale tip of his tongue flicked over his dry lips. Nelson, with a shrug of contempt, turned aside from him and signalled to two marines who stood close by.

"Take him to the punishment cells," he said. "And let him be chained. Mr. Scott—" (to his secretary, who stood forward immediately from the group close by) "—will you be good enough, Mr. Scott, to make a note of this conversation, and let an account be written out as soon as possible, so that I may deal with it when matters are less pressing."

Scott at once set to scribbling in a shorthand upon a tablet he held. I believe indeed, from something he told me later, that he did set out to make a narrative of what he had heard—and would that I possessed it to add to these our own poor accounts! But it was on his person when he was killed in the great battle now looming before us, and went overboard with his brave shattered body.

With Blackadder gone below, Nelson once more turned towards us.

"Gentlemen," he said abruptly, "I can, as you observe, offer you little choice. You have joined us, whether either of us likes it or no. And at this moment when you have joined us, we are on our way as we hope and believe to strike a blow at the sea-might of the enemy which will annihilate him utterly. I can promise you nothing but pain or death."

"They are enough, my lord," said Butterfield quietly; and Harry and I, beside him, murmured our own deep acquiescence.

And so, at the end, the great Admiral—the greatest of all time—turned away from us towards his officers again. But as he did so he hesitated once more and nodded towards the one member of our party who had stayed throughout in the background. McGuffie, his round face a study of a kind of melancholy apprehension, had done all in his power to make himself insignificant—a task impossible in the light of his massive bulk.

"And this man," said Nelson, "—this round fellow with the cutlass. Is he ours?—or theirs? You did not mention *him* in your account, Mr. Butterfield."

The lieutenant paused—and shuffled for a moment uncomfortably. When he spoke his face was suffused with a blush.

"A Scotsman, my lord. He—he helped us on our escape."

"Indeed?" And the keen eyes twinkled. "And was with you in the prison fortress, perhaps?"

Another hesitation; and then, as he saw a way out in ambiguity, the good Butterfield answered:

"Yes, my lord. He *was* with us in *La Grosse Tête*!"

"I see! A good servant of the King, in short!"

He suspected—I swear that he suspected. Butterfield coughed—and told, to my knowledge, his only great lie in all his life. He suddenly straightened himself and held up his head; and gabbled out:

"Habbakuk McGuffie, my Lord. Late merchant seaman. I impressed him in Dorset for His Majesty's Navy. He was captured as we were. I vouch for him and for his valour and loyalty."

Nelson, for the first time, smiled openly.

"So be it, Lieutenant. I take your word. Come, Hardy."

And he turned away again and so was gone. Behind me, I heard a vast sigh of relief from the Scot; and his murmur to Butterfield:

"Heaven bless ye, Lieutenant! Ye're a better man than me, sir!"

"McGuffie," hissed Butterfield, "—if you betray me after this I'll slit your rascally throat with that confounded whinger of yours, as you call it!"

"Amen," said McGuffie devoutly. "And I'd haud your jacket mysel' while ye did it! . . ."

On the Eve

And so we sailed south and further south. With us, as we went to join the fleet anchored off Cadiz in a blockade of the French, were the *Ajax* and the *Thunderer* and the frigate *Euryalus*. We were newly-painted all, in yellow and black, with white rings on the masts. And in the very air, it seemed, as we voyaged, there was the presage of great things growing—not a heart among us, humble or noble, but glowed with a strange exaltation.

We, for our part, were absorbed into the crew of the *Victory* herself. Harry and I shared space with some midshipmen in the cockpit and were fitted out with spare clothes from two boys of our own age. Butterfield lived in a cabin below the poop with the other officers. McGuffie went forward and shared with the carpenter, but we saw him often on the main deck or at gun drill below, and found him in a perpetual glow of delight, his old enmities over, his devotion entirely given now to the King whom once he had decried.

"It was just the way his Nainsel could talk," he once said. "Oh, he had a tongue on him like gold!—and I was aye easy swayed, easy swayed, Tam! When he ups wi' his tales o' Bonaparte and such, and what was sure to happen when he'd conquered England, I just drapped everything and followed him! I was daft—I was just daft! And me for the King a' the time, if I'd only kent! . . ."

As for Blackadder himself, we saw nothing of him. He was held close prisoner in a small dark cabin amidships in the gun deck. The marines who guarded him and took him his food told us he stayed silent, gazing eternally into the gloom, his face blank, only his eyes burning steadily with something of the old passion of fury as he looked up at their approach.

We learned from the other midshipmen something of the events of the past two years, while we had been out of all touch with the development of the war. From time to time, it is true, we had picked up news from prisoners brought in to join us at Tacoignières; but such reports were fragmentary and inadequate—now for the first time we had a coherent picture of what had been happening.

From the first, in those days of 1803 when we had been captured aboard the *Manon* and taken to France, Britain had feared invasion. It was known that Napoleon had an immense fleet of barges assembled at Boulogne—and not a coastguard along the southern shores of England but expected to see the black mass advancing one day through the morning mists. And behind Boulogne, ready to embark in the barges, were near two hundred thousand of villainous French troops—despoilers and ruffians, as we believed, but fine soldiers withal, and led by a man who was a genius, if an evil one.

A command of the sea was essential—upon that, for us, all depended. And on May 18 of 1803—the very day which showed us Abershaw as Blackadder, which began for Harry and me the whole adventure—Nelson hoisted his flag upon the *Victory* at Portsmouth and made sail for the Mediterranean. And the great blockade of the main French fleet began.

The months, the weary months went by with no action. Napoleon fretted impatiently, his desire being to assemble as many line-of-battle ships as he could in the Channel so as to cover the progress of the Great Invasion. And Nelson fretted too. We know, looking back in these after years, that although he gave no sign of it to us who were near him, he was an ailing and a despairing man in those long indecisive months of late 1804 and early 1805. His old eye wound was troubling him and he suffered pain incessantly from his arm, so badly amputated at Teneriffe. Above all, he despaired of ever forcing the French to battle—and he profoundly wanted to force the French to battle. He had, perhaps, a premonition that his life was moving towards its close, though he was barely forty-seven; and he longed to settle one way or the other with the old enemy before the end came—even, as happened in the event, while the end did come. . . .

Then at last, in March and April of the fated year of which I write, Admiral Villeneuve, at the peremptory command of his Emperor, stole out of Toulon and succeeded in beating unmolested through the Straits of Gibraltar—and forthwith disappeared, no man knew where! At least—one man knew where; or suspected where, with that instinctive genius for insight into his enemy's designs which was one of our great Nelson's most remarkable characteristics. The French were on their way across the Atlantic—to join the Spaniards, perhaps, in an attempt to destroy England on the circumference if not at the core—to capture and despoil our valuable possessions in the West Indies.

Basing all upon his instinct—facing the overwhelming responsibility of a move which no other British Admiral would ever have dared—Nelson set sail himself for the West. He was ill-supplied with provisions, his ships and men were worn out from the long spell at sea already; but still he went on—and with such rapidity and energy that he gained upon the French all the way, and they with near a month's good start. The news of the pursuit reached Villeneuve and filled him with despair. Above all men he feared and hated Nelson—would not face him; and so abandoned the campaign in the West and ignominiously set off to recross the Atlantic.

He made now for the Channel, so as to give Napoleon at last the opportunity to cross it. But Nelson was still in fast pursuit, and after an indecisive battle with Calder near Finisterre, the French Admiral lost heart entirely and made for Cadiz to rest his sick and weary men. Nelson had meantime landed himself at Gibraltar, and shortly afterwards made for England—where an immense reception awaited him for the daring and courage he had shown in the great Atlantic chase.

H.

But he had little time to enjoy his well-earned repose. Villeneuve was blockaded again by our fleet—this time at Cadiz. The moment for the final decisive action had come, and in September the greatest Admiral in all our history embarked once more at Portsmouth and headed south to take over the command. It was on this last voyage that we encountered him and were taken aboard the *Victory*; and so went forward ourselves to the battle which lingers still in my memory as the greatest, most tragic, yet most glorious experience I have ever known. . . .

Trafalgar

We joined the fleet under Vice-Admiral Collingwood on the 28th. It was evening, I recall—and the following day was Nelson's birthday. He took over his last command at the age of forty-seven.

To avoid arousing further apprehension in Villeneuve, safe tucked in Cadiz harbour, he forbade the firing of salutes or the hoisting of flags to notify his arrival. Yet all the vast fleet knew it, and a great glow and ripple of confidence and affection went through each man in every ship. Codrington (since Admiral Codrington, and my good friend) wrote: "Lord Nelson has arrived; a sort of general joy has been the consequence."

So, for a long month, we blockaded again—but in a desperate impatience. We knew the moment was ripe and over-ripe—the moment all the fleet, all England had waited for. We blockaded—but in a way to give the French all chance to put to sea. Our main body, including our *Victory* herself, stayed fifty miles off-shore and out of sight. Between us and the bay were only some small craft, watching and spying—ready to report the first signs of a move from the French and Spanish. The trap was prepared and baited: if only Villeneuve would sail!

Days, days, days. . . . And long impatient nights. We drilled, we fretted, we polished and repolished each article of armament—we drilled again and fretted again. For hours and weary hours Harry and I paced the main deck, silent of words but knowing each in his heart the tension growing up in the other. Butter-field, with us, fumed in an eternal longing for action—he who perforce had been held from action through all the two long years of the war already. And above us, on the quarter-deck, we saw our beloved commander pace also back and forth, his head lowered in converse with Hardy, or engaged in giving notes to Secretary Scott. And all the time a constant train of message bearers ran between us and the inshore frigates—and, as each one approached us, there was an eager showing of faces at every porthole and over every bulwark. Was the moment come?—was it come at last? . . .

The weather cleared—the painted ships shone out in all their glory of yellow and black. An off-shore breeze at times brought the scent of orange groves from Spain. And McGuffie, sharpening his whinger with an air of endless earnestness, solemn and solicitous, sang his eternal songs or recited the verses of his beloved Burns:

I am a son of Mars, who have been in many wars,
And show my cuts and scars wherever I come;
This here was for a wench, and that other in a trench,
When welcoming the French at the sound of the drum. . . .

And the carpenter and the bosun, and some nearby handful of the men with whom the irrepressible Scot had mated, would chant in a low determined murmur——

of the drum, of the drum! . . .

—rolling the r at the last in imitation of McGuffie's accent, yet in a way that came to have about it a terrible monotonous menace:

—oh, the drrrrum!

We know now, from all that has been written from a more intimate viewpoint since, of the deadly premonition growing up in the heart of our beloved commander in those final days of waiting. We know how he felt that he would never live through the great fight— how he made his will, how he wrote his last letters, how he prayed in the solitude of his cabin and so prepared himself. But in us, the men of his crew who loved him, there was no inkling—nothing but the gathering of courage from his very quiet presence above us on the quarter-deck, from his occasional words of cheerful confidence.

We waited—oh, we waited! Harry and I were cleared from the corner of the cockpit where we had bedded, so that the place could be prepared by the surgeons for the wounded we must needs anticipate (yet how could we know that the very spot upon which we had lain would be the bed of death on which the noblest of all would lie?) The decks were cleared, the planks scrubbed white, the great guns primed and polished. And the walls about the decks were painted scarlet. A colour strange indeed it seemed to us at the time—yet later, later, we knew too well why it was ever chosen! . . .

And at last, on the 19th of October, the message came. In fine weather and easterly, the Combined Fleet of the French and Spanish was coming out of port. The first of our commander's famous signals was hoist to the masthead: *General Chase, S.E.* A shout went up that rang through all the vibrant ship; and Nelson, on the poop, raised up his left arm to us in a gesture. . . .

Now all was an increase of activity. Men hurried to and fro securing lashings, testing tackles. Frigates assembled towards us with messages and drew away again towards the inshore squadron—firing as they went. And, as the day crept on, the picture grew more clear: one by one, and slowly in the little breeze, the ships of Villeneuve were creeping out of Cadiz and heading for Gibraltar.

All night the guns continued to sound as further messages came in—Bengal lights flared high and rockets soared in signals. By daylight on the twentieth we were near the mouth of the Straits ourselves in a fine sailing breeze that still was full of rain. Of Villeneuve there was still no sign—and as the day went forward we had news that he had altered course and was bearing northwards again. Northwards and westwards we went ourselves—then, in the night, the last of all, bore south-west again and finally stood to north-east. We, in that final dawn, peered out across the grey swelling ocean—crowded the decks and swarmed the nettings; and saw at last, in a final thrill, the looming shape of Cape Trafalgar and, before it, a ghostly train of ships—the enemy! And out upon the swelling sea went a great sigh and murmur of awe and huge relief.

So we advanced. The world knows now the master-plan our leader had devised which gave us victory—the design unprecedented and bold which split us into two lines advancing in a parallel to break the enemy's formation—the famous "Nelson touch" itself. At the time, we members of the crew knew nothing—except that the signals for division had been hoisted, and that the *Royal Sovereign* was to head one column, our very selves in the *Victory* the other. We sprang to obey all orders in a frenzy of eagerness—not one of us but longed for the moment of conflict. One of the midshipmen, with whom we had grown friendly, wrote down in a last letter to his parents the thoughts in each one of us: "We have just piped to breakfast. Thirty-five sails are now on our beam, about three miles off. Should I, my dear parents, fall in defence of my King, let that thought console you. I feel not the least dread on my spirits." He died in the battle, that boy—and it was I who took the sad unfinished little note from his pocket and sent it back to England when all was done. . . .

The wind was poor—we made a bare two knots. Yet at least we moved—we moved!—and as we moved the bands upon our decks played "Rule Britannia." In pride, in pomp, in circumstance, and with a sudden glow of golden sun across our flying colours, we drew nearer. Harry and I, in the crew of a gun on the quarter-deck, tied up our hair in kerchiefs. Our hearts beat uncontrollably, we trembled—yet in our spirits we were resolute. Close by, McGuffie, his round face pale for once, stood to attention with a priming rod before him—a grotesque of grotesques, but still in a shabby way glorious, as all were. Over from us, his sword at the ready, his eyes intent across the sea upon the enemy, was Butterfield—and in his set red face was a determination to avenge all that we had suffered in helplessness and inaction. To Blackadder, in chains below, we gave no thought—yet would that we had, as I realise now, looking back!—for even while we moved across the sullen sea that day—when the attention of every man upon the ship was elsewhere—the master-spy in his cell was fretting and chafing at the bonds that held him—had found a rough edge of nail in the bulkhead which acted as a file and with which he worked with all the will and resolution of his evil personality to free himself. . . .

As we went before the wind—as the line of battle shaped itself, it grew clear that at the outset we and the *Royal Sovereign* together would bear the whole brunt of the enemy's fire. Yet, if once we could weather it, if we could break through Villeneuve's crescent line and so cut his whole fleet apart, the day was won—our twenty-seven smaller ships against his thirty-three would gain the victory.

Our Admiral had gone below—as we established later, he was at this point writing his last prayer in his diary. Not long after eleven he came on the quarter-deck again and walked back and forth with Captain Blackwood. He was pale—but all about his frail person was that essence of greatness I have mentioned already. He was close to us, at about a quarter before noon, when he turned suddenly to Blackwood.

"One signal more, Blackwood," he said, "—there is time for one signal more."

"The whole fleet knows what is expected, my lord," replied the other. "There is no need for a further signal."

"I had meant something different, Blackwood—something personal, to wear away the irk of this long waiting."

He beckoned to Pasco, the signal officer, and instructed him to fly the flags for a signal to run:

"Nelson confides that every man will do his duty."

"Do you think it will hearten them, Lieutenant?" he added, turning to Butterfield, then close by his side.

"More, my Lord. It will inspire them. And yet—if I might make bold enough——"

"Speak on, man."

"We know, my Lord, of *your* confidence. We fight for you indeed, but our thoughts are with England also. England too confides."

"Done—done!" cried Nelson. "England confides! Pasco, send it so, do you see—*England* confides that every man will do his duty. And quickly, man—we engage close action any moment! "

And Pasco then, in deference, made the suggestion which cast the great signal in its final famous mould. There was a single group of flags for "expects," but the word "confides" would have to be spelt out letter by letter. Did the Admiral think, perhaps, that to save time——

"Best—best of all! " Lord Nelson cried. And Pasco ran to execute the command—and a moment later, when the array fluttered out at the masthead, there was a huge wild cheer from every ship in the lines behind; and simultaneously, to starboard, we heard the first far thunder of the enemy guns as the *Sovereign* under Collingwood drove into the crescent line. . . .

And now for a space my memory is a turmoil and confusion. I recall that silence fell again as we drew nearer ourselves—was aware of no more than the creaking of the blocks all about my head, the flap of the loose sails in the little wind. And then, a quarter of a mile away, there was a puff of smoke across the water from a great Frenchman—the *Bucentaure* herself, perhaps. The whistle of shot overhead, the crash as it tore the rigging. . . . Blackwood went to the side, leaving his commander for his own ship; and as he went Nelson said to him: "God bless you, Blackwood, I shall never speak to you again."

We thought it nothing—the natural premonition of any man before battle. And all thoughts on the remark in any case were stifled in the sudden din that now broke forth. We were among them. A shot rent through our main top-gallant sail—and an instant later the massed guns of the enemy line before us—400 as we reckoned thereafter—roared in on us a merciless torrent of fire.

That we survived that first wild onslaught is a marvel. Our decks were swept—our dead slithered here and there, contorted and mutilated. The air was full of the screams of the wounded and dying—I saw why all the walls were scarletted! I saw Mr. Scott, the secretary, blasted near in two with a ball from Nelson's very side—and sickened as McGuffie and an officer of marines dragged the streaming body to the bulwark and cast it over.

Again and again the fire was repeated. We lay upon the decks, the surgeons and their officers moving among us, hurrying the wounded below to the cockpit. And still we held our own fire—until we should be in the veriest thick. And behind us, calmly, calmly, walked Neson, Hardy by his side—and both at stroll as if upon a pleasure cruise! A jag of flying shot caught Hardy's foot, and he stayed for a moment looking down at it, in a surprise near comical.

"This is too warm, Hardy, to last long!" said his leader—and resumed his walk. . . .

My ears were deafened in the monstrous din—my throat parched—I could not utter. Harry, beside me on the deck, had gone white—his eyes stared out in a nausea at the welter of blood surrounding. A severed arm lay beside us, where it had been lopped from the body of a marine—and the frozen hand still held the barrel of a shattered musket. . . .

But now at last, when all seemed past endurance, when the torrent of fire against us had reached its full fury and it seemed we could not last another instant—now at last, when we were in the deepest midst and had almost cut the line, the order came to loose our own fire. We thrust the matches in the guns, and at a distance of thirty feet, blasted full in the stern of the French flagship with all our battery. The sound of splintering wood, of wild crashing, of agonised screaming, rang out above the sound of the firing itself. The air was full of smoke and swirling dust—we choked and stifled. But in a moment's sudden clearing we saw that the stern of the *Bucentaure* was blown to pieces—was shattered almost all away.

Confusion mounted. Behind us, our column was flying too in the enemy's midst. As we learned later, the *Sovereign*, at the head of our second column southwards, was through the line. We fired and fired again, until I felt my head a huge dull vibration. I could no longer hear—saw only imperfectly from streaming eyes. For an instant McGuffie loomed out of the swirling smoke. He bled from a wound above his eye—had swathed his head in a bright yellow cloth; but his face was red again and smiling.

"A McGuffie, a McGuffie," he yelled in the din—and charged forward into the smoke towards the bulwark, his whinger whirling overhead. For by now we had grappled with the great *Redoubtable*—were locked in a forest of masts and a tangle of lines and netting, our guns on the lower decks nose to nose and blasting; and hand to hand fighting was going forward across the outer rails. And still, behind us, calmly walking, an encouragement to all in those moments of death and terror, went those two tranquil figures side by side. . . .

And so the climax came—the battle mounted and the climax came. High above us, seen in ragged glimpses through the smoke, were the French sharp-shooters in the three high tops of the *Redoubtable*. They raked our decks with musket fire and pistols—even grenades. The little figure on the quarter-deck, his decorations at his breast, was conspicuous—towards him, above all others, they aimed. In a moment's lull I heard Hardy plead with him to cover his stars with a kerchief. But he shook his head and smiled—and still walked calmly among us.

And then——

And before then——

Death and Victory

I was aware, in a moment of nightmare, of Butter-field looming close to me out of the smoke. His face was wild and smeared all over in blood. He mouthed at me in the din, but for a moment I heard nothing; and when I did it was only in broken fragments. But the news was enough to set my heart pounding even further.

"Blackadder! Devil take it, Tom—Blackadder! . . ."

I gaped forward to where he pointed with his sword; and saw on the instant, on the main deck below, our enemy. His black hair flying, his cloak about him, he strode forward. At his wrist was the filed fragment of the manacle that had held him. In one white hand was a pistol he had snatched from a body on the deck, in the other, glinting red, was a cutlass. And his face as he came was the face of a man gone beyond all sanity at last.

We stood for an instant paralysed at the sudden apparition. The madman before us clambered and leapt—and was upon the quarter-deck before us. He swayed for a moment against the rail—and raised his pistol to point at Harry's breast at last. His lips writhed—no sound came out of them; but I knew he meant to say:

"The boy! I will have the boy!"

With a sudden great convulsion of movement Butterfield acted. He lunged sideways and sent Harry spinning and tumbling across the corpse of a gunner sprawled out on the deck at our feet. Simultaneously, something flashed like a jag of lightning across the deck before us. It was McGuffie's whinger—he coming on us through the smoke and throwing it from where he stood. Its razor edge caught Blackadder's hand at the moment when he fired. The shot went wide—went screaming past my ear. The pistol clattered to the deck. And the spy, still holding his arm outstretched before him, gazed for an instant foolishly at the two streaming stumps of his thumb and forefinger, carried away by the deadly weapon as it struck.

Then he screamed—and the sound, shearing through all else in the din, froze the very blood at my heart. He leapt forward, slashing with his cutlass. I felt a burning pain at my ear and across my shoulder—and stumbled backwards and fell on the hot wet deck.

McGuffie by this time had sprung forward himself, and he and Butterfield between them grappled with the spy's great figure. The Scotsman, his mouth pouring blood from a blow from the cutlass hilt, grasped upwards and with a mighty effort wrenched Blackadder's weapon away. Yet in the effort he weakened his balance, and the spy, with a huge convulsion, shook both him and Butterfield loose and stumbled forward, slithering on the streaming blood which covered all.

Harry lay half-stunned where he had fallen under Butterfield's saving blow. In an instant the spy was atop him. With a maniac gesture he tore at Harry's shirt—ripped it open as if to assure himself in his madness that the tattoo mark was still upon his breast. Its bright and livid colours were revealed—and with a howl of triumph the enemy straightened himself, Harry's slender body grasped at his breast in a monstrous caricature of the attitude of a mother with her child.

He staggered forward to the bulwark rail—to the point where we interlocked still with the *Redoubtable*. His back was towards us as he went and at it, aiming hastily but straightly, Butterfield fired. A spurt of blood stained out at the shoulder—another an instant later as Butterfield seized up a second musket and fired again. But still the vast black crooked shape went forward.

At the rail he turned. By now he gripped Harry's body with one arm only, the boy still stunned—his

face a white patch against the sable cloak. The enemy
stooped and dragged a musket from the arm of a
corpse that sagged at the bulwarks. Then, with an
effort superhuman, he clambered on the rail itself and
stood erect and swaying there before us.

All this I saw from the deck to which I had fallen.
But now I struggled upright and seized the nearest
weapon—the very pistol that Blackadder himself had
dropped. McGuffie too was on his feet and rushing
forward. Butterfield stayed motionless, afraid to fire
again lest he should strike Harry.

I threw the heavy pistol with all my strength. It
caught the spy on the shoulder. He reeled—he must
have weakened much by now from the wounds in his
back. He loosened his grasp on Harry—and at the
moment McGuffie was upon him. A smoke wreath
covered them—for a space I saw nothing; and when
it cleared the Scotsman, grasping Harry, was huddled
at the rail, the spy's tall shape above him. As I looked
he drove downward with his boot in McGuffie's face;
but the blow glanced and the Scotsman, still gripping
Harry, rolled sideways and fell to the deck—but was
safe and alive, as I saw from the sudden blank innocent
smile he gave before he toppled to unconsciousness.

As for the spy—for one statuesque moment he stayed
poised on the high rail; then, with a sudden surge of
wild last energy, grasped at the rigging above and
clambered aloft towards the tops. Like an evil bird he
mounted through the smoke until he was high above
our heads, we staring upwards after him. Once he
stumbled and nearly fell as he grasped at a line with his

mutilated hand. His face was icy and white—it was the face of a man already dead. But still he climbed. . . .

And now, at the end of all, what can I say? Through the years I have speculated—and in my heart I do not know the truth. I can vouch for no more than what I saw. It may have been—it *may*. . . . I know nothing— nothing!——

Only that I saw Blackadder pause at last. He stayed outstretched against the rigging. In his hand he held still the musket he had snatched. He grasped it now at his shoulder, somehow, and levelled it at Butterfield. He fumbled with his bleeding finger stumps at the trigger. He swayed—he almost fell. And then it was as if a last evil thought came into him—and with a glow of ineffable triumph and rage on his face, he swung the musket suddenly away—and aimed it now, no longer at Butterfield, but at the small calm figure of the Admiral. From the angle of his fire he was in a direct line with the angle of fire from the sharpshooters beyond him in the French tops. How do I know what ball it was that struck at last?—his, or one of theirs?

The spy did fire at least—and the musket fell from his hands. I heard a sudden cry from the quarter-deck behind. I turned—and saw our beloved Admiral on his knees, one hand touched the deck. Hardy was forward on the instant and had bent over him. And I heard, in a sudden stillness, the quiet sad voice:

"They have done for me at last, Hardy. Oh, my backbone is shot through! . . ."

Simultaneously Butterfield, beside me, fired too— and upwards. Dazed, incomprehending, sick at heart,

I gazed aloft again. A stain of red spread over the evil face far far above—we saw no more the countenance which once we had known as the gentle countenance of Mr. Abershaw. A last cry, forlorn, half-pathetic even at that moment of moments, came down to us through the din new-raging. And the great black crooked figure fell—soared outwards like the malignant bird it had ever resembled; and plunged between the grappling ships; and sank in the blood-red sea. . . .

The rest is history and known to all the world.

We carried our beloved Nelson below, his poor white face all covered with a kerchief; and he was laid in the berth in the cockpit where Harry and I ourselves had rested. All around were other wounded men and dying; but at the sight of him, in all their agony, a deep sad sigh went trembling in the fetid air.

His clothes were removed, his frail warped body swathed in a sheet. We brought refreshing drinks at the hurried whispered orders of Dr. Beatty, who tended him. We hoped against all hope as we crowded there that the wound was not mortal. But in his own valiant heart he knew that all was over.

"You can do nothing for me, Beatty," he sighed. "Nothing, nothing. . . ."

Above, the battle raged still; but victory was ours— had been ours foretold from long before he fell. At the grappled bulwarks hand-to-hand fighting went on —grenades hailed down from the *Redoubtable's* tops. But the *Temeraire*—the fighting *Temeraire*, next to our own the most famous ship in all that fearful battle

—drew in on the Frenchman's other side, and she was beaten. She struck her colours—and the day was won.

On all sides else we likewise met with victory—ship after ship of the enemy surrendered; and by two o'clock the issue was in no further doubt. Hardy, coming down from the weltering decks, was able to report it so to his beloved leader; and with a sigh, in the very chill of death itself, he turned his head and whispered:

"I have done my duty. God be praised."

Later still, shortly after four, when it was clear from all above that the sea-power of Napoleon had been broken for ever, he asked Hardy, his dearest friend of all those close to him there, to kiss him; which he did in sorrow—then turning away, with his hand upon his eyes, to hide his noble feeling. Nelson sighed again, and murmured, at the end of all, "God and my country"; and so died, at the height of his moment of greatness. And we, who lingered around him, men weathered in battle and tempered in every last reach of human suffering, wept to see him, and stayed upon our knees to pray.

With Harry, recovered now from his experience, but pale and sad of eye, I stood in a corner of the gloomy cockpit. My own slight wound at the ear from our enemy's sword was bandaged over—ached still a little, but was as nothing to the deep empty burning in my heart. Beside us, in a little interval from his duties above, was Lieutenant Butterfield, his head bowed down, his hands close clasped in prayer on the hilt of his sword. And at the door for a moment, looking in upon us, was McGuffie, his round cheeks wet with tears. He hobbled badly from his injury in the last fight with the spy, and his teeth at the front were gone. He opened his mouth to speak, but no words came. He trembled at the lip and turned away.

We were safe—we all were safe, our long adventure over. But no joy shone in us; we looked upon the silent figure, the figure of the noblest Englishman we had ever known, perhaps the greatest sailor in all the world's long history—we looked on him, so still in death and glory, and we sorrowed.

We went above at last, and walked the tragic decks of our rent and tattered ship. About us heaved the eternal ocean; and somewhere in its depths, his evil courses run, was the lost unhappy man we had known as Blackadder.

ENVOI

by

THE EDITOR

AND SO the adventure ended—the adventure which had begun so many months before on that May day of 1803 when Tom Cathro and Harry Rowan went down to the sea at Lytchett and found the little empty tossing cask that once had held Moonshine. Between that moment and their arch-enemy's final plunge into the sea at Trafalgar, they had lived through storm and shipwreck, pursuit and danger; had been imprisoned and submitted to torture; had escaped and flown across France in a balloon; had finally come face to face with death in the greatest sea battle in the history of Europe.

It remains now, in this brief closing section, for me as editor to tie the few last threads and so take the tale of *Blackadder* to its conclusion.

Lord Nelson died at half-past four on that fatal October day of 1805—barely five hours after the start of the battle. An hour later the fighting ended—there was one last reverberating explosion as the French ship *Achille* blew up; then silence fell across the wreckage-stewn sea and in the first shades of night the losses were counted and the full extent of the great Admiral's victory assessed.

Our fleet had gone into battle with twenty-seven ships. We suffered some 400 killed and 1,200 wounded. The combined French and Spanish fleets had mustered some thirty-three ships. Eleven of these retired to Cadiz, broken and distressed; four stayed at sea and were captured a few days later by a roving British squadron; the remaining eighteen struck colours to us during the battle itself. The Spaniards lost 1,000 men killed and some 1,400 wounded; the French— the great host upon which Napoleon had counted so fiercely—had some 1,200 wounded and almost three times that number killed: 3,373 as the final computation ran. Over and above, many prisoners were taken from the captured vessels. . . . Thus the sea-power of Bonaparte was shattered indeed for ever; gone were all hopes of an invasion of England.

On the night of the battle, and for two days thereafter, a great gale blew in from the west. In its mournful rage about the wounded ships it seemed to echo the great sorrow in every British heart as the news of the death of the commander-in-chief ran through the fleet. Men wept. Great Collingwood wrote: "My heart is rent with the most poignant grief"; and a young sailor—an ordinary seaman of the *Royal Sovereign*—said in a letter home: "Our dear Admiral Nelson is killed! so we have paid pretty sharply for licking 'em. I never set eyes on him, for which I am both sorry and glad; for to be sure I should like to have seen him—but then, all the men in our ships who have seen him are such soft toads they have done nothing but blast their eyes and cry ever since he was killed.

God bless you! chaps that fought like the devil sit down and cry like a wench! . . ."

The world knows how the body of this man so beloved of all was brought home through the storm. As it lay in state in the Painted Hall at Greenwich, the whole of Britain mourned. The torn fragments of the flags of the *Victory* were placed upon the coffin, which then was taken in procession up the Thames to Whitehall. From there, it went through the streets of London, amid a great crowd of sorrowing onlookers; and Viscount Nelson was laid to rest at last by the flickering light of many torches in St. Paul's.

In that procession, walking with the other sailors from the flagship, went our own four friends—Tom and Harry side by side, with Butterfield forward a little among the officers and McGuffie behind with the carpenters and bosun's mates. When all was over they met together and loitered in a close silence through the deserted streets. Their hearts were full—of sorrow for the death of their great leader, of joy and thanksgiving for their own deliverance. Only once did they mention that other who had also died at Trafalgar—who also held a place in their hearts, but a place of despicable, not honourable memory.

"Aye, aye," said McGuffie, sighing, "—his Nainsel too! He was a bad, bad man—I should never have paid heed to him. His Nainsel too awa'! Ye know, I wonder——"

He broke off; and all four looked at each other in silence. But each knew what the others were thinking. Had it been, after all, the shot from Blackadder's gun which had found its billet in the small frail figure pacing the quarter-deck of the *Victory*? Or, as history supposes, had it been a ball from the mizzen-top of the French *Redoubtable*? They never knew; and in all the years to come they kept the speculation silent among themselves, until long afterwards Admiral Cathro committed to paper his own description of the battle of Trafalgar as you have read it.

A few days after the funeral the four friends journeyed to Dorset; and towards the end of January of the year 1806 they were reunited with the others who had taken part in the great adventure with them. The old Chevalier was still frail and distressed from the bitterness of his experience at the Palace of Rohan-Soubise and the exposure of the cross-Channel voyage in the fishing-smack. But he had been well-tended through the months by Mignonne, who, with Blue Nose, had taken up residence in the little manor house at Lytchett. Blue Nose, once he had seen his charges safe home, had journeyed to Portsmouth to report once more for service; but the wound he had received from Blackadder's gun on the French shore had re-opened, and so he was sent back to Dorset. Even now he was still a sick man, but slowly recovering, and able to help Mignonne with little tasks about the house.

In the joy of seeing his beloved grandson again, the Chevalier improved too in his health, and within a month was able to rise from his bed and to walk in the garden. And it was there, one early evening in spring, that he told the assembled friends at last the full story of the Treasure of the de Rohans which had so impelled the evil imagination of their ancient enemy.

The Treasure, it seemed, a great hoard of gold and silver and precious stones, had been bequeathed to the Chevalier's branch of the family some two-and-a-half centuries before by an Italian nobleman whose life had been saved by a de Rohan during the ill-fated Last Crusade of Don John of Austria. It had been hidden away by that early de Rohan to be used by the family only in need; and the tradition grew that the secret of its whereabouts should be known only to he head of the house, to be passed on by him to the heir on his deathbed. At the time of the Revolution, when the Chevalier was fleeing before the menace of *La Vipère Noire*, he removed the Treasure from its hiding place beneath the palace and concealed it elsewhere. Reaching England, he determined to leave a clue to its whereabouts. He believed (as indeed proved to be the case) that some of his old enemies might still be pursuing him, and so did not wish to give Harry the responsibility of knowing fully where the Treasure lay while he was still a child—and yet he felt he had to give his grandson some indication, as the last of the line, so that he could reclaim his rightful inheritance when all was over. In his distress (and remember that he was a man sick in mind as well as body after the trials of the escape), he conceived the strange idea of having the clue tattooed on Harry's breast. It was his intention, he explained, to tell Harry later what the design meant, or to leave a full account of its purpose among his papers if he himself should die in the interval.

Thus the enigmatic emblem above Harry's heart. The crest itself was identical with the crest main in the great hall at Rohan-Soubise; the network of lines behind it, each inscribed with a small figure, indicated the paths to be taken from the crest to where the Treasure lay—so many metres back in a direct line, so many to the left, so many then to the right, and so on; until, in the words of the inscription in ancient French above and below the whole design——

That which was hidden will be found at last:
And he who bears the name I bear
Will come unto his own.

And so that night in the garden, surrounding the noble figure of the old aristocrat, the friends swore that when all was over, when the war was won and it was possible once more to move freely in France, they would journey together to Rohan-Soubise, where they had suffered such bitter torment in the past, and find and claim the Treasure for its true owners.

How they did so in the fullness of time (for it was not until after 1815, when Napoleon met his final defeat at Waterloo, that it was possible for them to go), is another story. It will be sufficient to say here that the finding of the Treasure, concealed, as it happened, not far from the spot from which the balloon had soared, was not achieved without much danger—once more Tom Cathro and Harry de Rohan were involved in adventure, which, if it did not bring them face to face with another Blackadder, led them to an encounter with a villain almost as malignant: the son, in the event, of that grim lieutenant of *La Vipère Noire* who had died on the beach at Carteret—Louis Kabal.

The tale of that second great adventure may be told some other time. It ended with the claiming of the Treasure indeed; and with it, after all his wanderings, Harry was able to found the great business of Rowan and Sons, of London, the fame of which lingers to this day. The old Chevalier, alas, did not live to enjoy the final triumph; he died at the age of eighty-five in the very year of Waterloo itself, and was buried in the little churchyard of Lytchett, where his grave may still be seen.

Of the others in our own present tale, Lieutenant Butterfield rejoined the Navy and was carving for himself a career of the greatest distinction when he was killed in the ill-fated Walcheren Expedition of 1809. This too is another story, some fragments of it already written down indeed by Tom Cathro, who was at Butterfield's side when he fell. He, as we know, joined the Navy too; and became, in due course, and after a long and distinguished service, Admiral Sir Thomas Cathro. A sketch of his later life, with some account of the early adventures described in this book, appears in an issue of the *Naval Chronicle* of 1868, the year following his quiet death in retirement at Lytchett.

Mignonne stayed on with the de Rohans in the manor house, helping to look after the old Chevalier, who had come to be devoted to her. The friendship between her and Harry ripened into love; and with his grandfather's blessing they were married in 1814, thereafter sharing a long and happy life together surrounded by their family, until they died within a week of each other in 1862.

Blue Nose never fully recovered from his wound and retired from the sea. He had no people of his own, and so stayed on near the de Rohans in Dorset, in the very cottage which had once belonged to the widow Cathro—the cottage from the window of which Tom had had his first apprehensive glimpse of Blackadder, in the days when he had seemed no more than the leader of the old Loblolly Boys.

As for McGuffie—with the adventure over he became a changed man. He quietened a little in manner and took to religion. He made a pilgrimage to Lanark to see his old mother, who still lived, and then returned south to join the Navy with Tom and Butterfield, so serving the King he had once so eloquently despised. He distinguished himself greatly by his courageous action off-shore at Corunna—was wounded there and given a small pension. He travelled with Tom and Harry to France and took part in the adventure which befell in the course of the finding of the Treasure; and thereafter, retiring in his age from all active life, he took up residence in the cottage at Lytchett which had belonged in the old times to "Mr. Abershaw." He devoted himself to good works and, by a strange stroke of irony, set to keeping pigeons in the old cotes about the house which still stood. But——

"Ah, they're different birds these, my lads!" he

would say, "—real different from them his Nainsel kept! Bonny wee things—oh, bonny! Come on, come on, my hinnies! Here's auld Habbie wi' yer dinner! —come on, come on!—and never mind what that auld villain used tae use ye for; it's a' gone by and past— ye're just my bonny hinnies now, and an auld man's comfort. . . ."

He also, by a final irony, took to playing the flute; and his favourite air, despite all past associations, was the Serenade by Haydn which Tom and Harry had heard as boys that night of nights on the beach when they almost met their deaths. So it was that in the years before the old Scotsman died, Tom Cathro, visiting Lytchett and passing the cottage of a summer night, would hear the old air drifting out to him. And the years would roll away and he would fancy himself a boy again, with the adventure all before him. He would feel once more the chill of terror which had struck through him the night he saw Blackadder for the first time; for a moment his memory would surge with the recollection of the great storm in the Channel which they had ridden out in the longboat; he would experience for an instant on his cheek the ghostly caress of the winds of heaven as he and his companions soared aloft from the grounds of Rohan in the balloon. . . . And then he would smile in the sudden recollection that it was not Abershaw who played, but harmless McGuffie; and go on his way to the old manor house which Harry had made over to him as his own property to live in on his spells of shore leave and to retire to when all was done.

Only once, on one such evening, as he walked beyond McGuffie's cottage towards the beach, with the sound of the Serenade in his ears and the soft cooing of the pigeons mingling—only once did he know a moment of real fear again. In the gathering dusk, as he walked, it seemed to him that there was a whispering of long leather boots through the grasses. In the uncertain light he thought he saw the sudden gleam of a cutlass. And on the headland above the cove, dim and awesome in the moonlight, he seemed to glimpse a tall black figure, the hands outstretched and raised to the sky in a gesture of unholy rage. . . .

He stopped in his tracks, his heart beating; and then in a moment the imaginary vision faded and he was himself again. But it was later that night, sobered and full of old memories, that he wrote in a letter to a friend that paragraph with which I opened this book, and with which I now end it:

" . . . *I have seen much, I have done much; I have adventured in foreign lands and upon the high seas; I have been within a sight of death and wrestled with fear itself. But in all my long days of travel and travail I have known no such terror as gripped me in the heart long ago—long ago when I was a boy; and I encountered for the first time, face to face, the monstrous figure we knew as Blackadder. . . .*"

Here ends his story: the story of *La Vipère Noire*, evil of memory, who knew no mercy, whose heart was dark with hate against all men; and whose crooked shape indeed, they say, can still be glimpsed upon the headland at Lytchett on stormy cloud-racked nights, the arms upflung to the sky, the white face twisted in an eternal rage.

Here ends his story. And the story of those who so gallantly opposed him; and finally, at the moment of his last great evil act—the wickedest of all—destroyed him.

THE END